N[

BE ENCOUNTERED

NUDISTS MAY

BE ENCOUNTERED

MARY SCOTT

Library of Congress Catalog Card Number: 90–60285

British Library Cataloguing in Publication Data
Scott, Mary
  Nudists may be encountered.
  I. Title II. Series
  823: 914[F]

  ISBN 1–85242–173–8

First published 1991 by
Serpent's Tail, 4 Blackstock Mews, London N4

Set in 10/12.5pt Walbaum by Selectmove Ltd, London

Printed on acid-free paper by
Nørhaven A/S, Viborg, Denmark

Contents

NUDISTS MAY
BE ENCOUNTERED

What went with what? Who was she today? And why? Naked, Julia stretched under the sheet, stretched so hard she pulled her stomach muscles to their full length. With each day she spent in the sun these crucial questions mattered less.

Each evening, arriving at a new hotel, she carried from the car one suitcase, one shoulder bag, a striped beach bag and a Guernsey knotted round her shoulders. Each morning she opened all her luggage, looked at the shirts and dresses and pairs of trousers, felt a moment's regret for a favourite red silk blouse, before choosing either the cotton shorts and the yellow tee shirt or the denim shorts and the pink top.

Sometimes she walked miles along the clifftops, taking no notice of the scenery. Sometimes she stopped for hours to gaze across the sea, to peer between rocks, to watch an osprey ride the thermals. Sometimes she ran – through the rare rain or to feel the wind on her face.

It was a just over a week since she had first set foot on the Dorset coast path. Each night she spoke to a waiter to order a meal; each morning she asked for boiled rather than scrambled eggs for breakfast. Otherwise she could not remember when she had last spoken to anyone. There was only the sun, the seaweed, the feel of pebbles, sand or shingle under her feet and a night asleep in a hotel room. So it was a shock this morning, after miles of deserted sands, to come into a small crowded bay: to see buckets and spades and sandcastles, a parade of shops with fishing nets and beach balls and to return to a world of people.

She picked her way between them, treading with care so as not to shower things with sand. A woman she passed was telling her husband to put on his shirt or he would burn. She watched a wet swimsuit twisted from the body of a screaming toddler, and a beach towel making freakish shapes as the woman under it changed.

Julia turned away from the sea, stepped from sand onto concrete and settled herself at a terrace table outside a café. She ordered a pot of tea for one. She put on her sunglasses to decrease her visibility, but she could still see something of herself; brown knees, frayed cut-offs. What kind of statement did she think she made?

It was certainly not one of the many studied effects which Paul had variously condemned as 'ludicrous', 'over the top', 'outrageous', 'dingy', or – most damaging of all – 'silly'. How often had this meant an edgy evening, when she had been unable to concentrate on what people were saying because of an ill-placed fabric rose or an over-embroidered antique shawl? Sometimes she was so brought down by one of his pronouncements that she had to change completely. And then, because her first effort had been wrong, it was hard to know, now, if or when she was ready.

'Paul, what do you think of this? Is it all right?'

'Of course it is. How much longer are you going to be? Anyway, no one will notice.' That always made her reach, in agitation, for something else, so that when they finally set off she was already exhausted and Paul was angry and full of contempt.

'You know how it is,' he would say to their hosts, on the pretext of apologising for arriving late, 'She couldn't find a thing to wear. You should see the state of the bedroom. It took her two hours to come up with that.'

'You look lovely whatever you wear, Julia,' someone would say.

It turned out Paul had been wrong. The fact was that she had achieved something. Won a national competition – well a competition in a national magazine – by imagining how to put together three exceptional outfits for three occasions: a job interview, meeting a partner's parents for the first time, and addressing a conference.

The competition set a fairly tight budget so Julia decided to mix second-hand clothes with new ones. For the interview she opted for a cream silk shirt, and a tailored black skirt. That would show she could fit in neatly anywhere. She added something for the panel to remember her by – sheer seamed black tights with black and grey checked flat shoes and, on the lapel of her jacket, a blue glass antique brooch. Her bag was also a surprise – a black purse sewn over with tiny blue beads and a thin, black shoulder strap. The brooch and the bag would make it clear she had originality although, taken in the context of the rest of the outfit, not too much.

On a first visit to a partner's parents, she decided, she would want to make it clear that her relationship was primarily with him, not them. The ensemble should, of course, not be too sexy, but polite, though not conciliatory – nothing that could suggest an inclination to join his mother in the kitchen to whip up a batch of fairy cakes. It should be slightly, but only very slightly, bizarre and unmistakably modern. That meant trousers. She hit upon a pair of corduroy breeches which would fit snugly at the waist but balloon over the hips, with highly-polished brown leather boots for a touch of chic, a maroon Italian sweater, which at 15p at a jumble sale had been a real snip, and a jaunty maroon beret.

The conference was easier. She didn't have to worry what happened from the waist down as this would be hidden by the table holding her notes. Other than that, it was important that she should look interesting so that even if what she said was dull the audience would not be bored; that the outfit should take account of the long range view – jewellery or other small items were irrelevant – and that it should draw attention to her face.

She defined the waist with a wide black leather belt, studded with silver. The lines of the top must be simple, but eye-catching; she chose an emerald, short-sleeved sweater. Over it, for dramatic effect, an old school blazer into which she would sew shoulder pads to make the silhouette wider. No need for a hat, but the hair must be pulled off the face to minimise distraction and caught at the nape in a black band into which she would stick a single green feather. That way, every time she turned her head to address one section of the audience, the rest of them would have something to be surprised about.

Julia tried it all out in the bedroom mirror. She put a table in front of her to see how she would look from the lecture hall. It was unfortunate that Paul came home just then. His reaction might have been enough to make her call a halt to the whole thing. He was particularly scathing about the feather, which she immediately agreed to be a mistake. But she could do nothing about it. She had been 'carried away' as Paul had put it. She had already posted the entry.

'You were wrong,' she said to Paul, when her prize of two hundred pounds arrived.

'I suppose you're going to spend it on even more clothes.'

'No. I'm going away. For two weeks I think.'

She packed a selection of outfits and drove south because it was the quickest way out. Once clear of London she stopped, consulted the *AA Handbook* and wondered, where next?

'Dorset,' someone had said at a recent dinner. 'Wonderful place for a short break. Absolutely unspoilt. Spectacular scenery.' So here she was.

She had been lucky with the weather. It was taking a risk, when she thought about it, to go to the seaside in September. She stretched her legs under the table, feeling the same satisfaction that she felt when she woke that morning. What went with what no longer mattered. She wanted instead to wear fewer and fewer clothes, to have next to nothing left between her and the sun: to take off her shorts and let the sun's rays reach the tops of her thighs. She jerked out of the café chair, paid for the tea and strode away from the crowd. In pursuit of pleasure, not effect.

She settled on a slab of rock with her shorts rolled into a pillow. That was better. But her breast felt shifty under the pink top. She sat up and looked around. Further away the cliffs were higher, the strip of rocks narrower. She hurried to the far end of the bay where the sun gazed from above the cliff with hot, friendly passion. No one else was around. Turning her back on the distant crowd, she sat and unbuttoned her top. She tipped her face up to the sun. But she was soon uncomfortable. She could not turn round or lie down. Someone might see and this was not Brighton and there were families about.

She buttoned up, put on her shorts, slung her bag over her shoulder and walked to the edge of the sea, then back again. She walked past the crowded beach and the café. She walked on and on, imagining herself utterly alone wearing nothing at all.

When she next looked inland, the terrain had changed to soft, silvery sand and rustling, bumpy dunes. Half-way between the dunes and the water stood a green sign, a foot high, no more. She squatted down to read it, balancing on the balls of her feet. On this part of the beach, she read, 'Nudists May Be Encountered.'

Nudists. People with no clothes on. She could lie in the sun; the wind could blow all over her, even, with careful positioning, the neglected places under her arms.

She found, as she walked on, that this place, like any other, had its etiquette. People in swimsuits or shorts and tops strolled at liberty on the wide sands. The unclothed, except when swimming, stayed in the background, secluded in the lee of a dune. Finally she found an unoccupied hollow. She dropped to her knees. Tumbled out of her clothes.

She lay, as she had envisaged, on her back. Heat sank unopposed through her skin. A kaleidoscope of colour shifted behind her closed eyelids. Perhaps she was asleep. Or perhaps she was awake?

She made no effort to turn over, although she thought about it, imagined how it might be to lean on one elbow, to twist her body in a single movement. Instead she opened her eyes and watched a small cloud move across the sky. When it had gone she turned to watch the white waves roll up the beach then roll back. Closer, there were her outstretched fingers to study as they burrowed through the sand.

Her cheeks, her stomach, her arms and her lower legs felt heavy, pressed under the weight of the sun, then light and drifting in its warmth.

Hours could have passed. She sat up. Others around her were standing, stretching, trying the water, strolling through the dunes.

Apart from one plump couple, they were all men. Nude but not naked. They wore things. Things which left their genitals exposed. One man had a rucksack, another a white cotton hat, a third an unbuttoned shirt, a fourth, sandshoes. It was, she supposed, a reduction of clothes to pure function – to protect one's head, back or feet from summer's elements.

Her own body was nearly ready again for clothes. She felt tired, even exhausted from the powerful attentions of the sun. And it was time to find a hotel.

'Would you talk to me for a few minutes?' A red nude man with black hair. A bag, no other accessories.

'I was about to go.'

'Just for a few minutes. It'd make my day.'

She glanced at her watch. 'All right.'

'Are you a naturist?'

'I don't know.'

'You don't mind me being like this?' He waved his hand in the direction of his lower half.

'Not at all.'

'You mean you *are* a naturist?'

'I don't know. I like taking my clothes off in the sun.'

'May I sit down?' He did so. There was a moment's pause.

'Your skin hasn't a single blemish,' he said. 'This is like Paradise. I never imagined this would happen. To sit like this with such a beautiful woman. What more could any man ask?'

'I don't know.'

People with clothes on strolled by.

'Paradise.' he said again. 'So many people misunderstand what naturism is about.'

'I expect so.'

'The innocence. You've no idea what this means to me. You and I. Here. Like Adam and Eve.' He extracted a small, oddly-shaped, yellow and white stone from the bag at his feet and offered it to her. 'Unusual, isn't it? I found it further down the beach. Feel how smooth it is.'

'It looks it.'

She took out her Ambre Solaire and rubbed a small amount on her nose.

'Could I borrow some?' He turned sideways, lying full length. 'My stern,' tapping his buttocks, 'can't take too much sun.'

She handed him the tube, being fairly and correctly sure he would not ask her outright to rub it in for him.

They were sitting on opposite sides of the small hollow. She gazing at the sea, he at her.

'Would you sit closer?' he asked, smoothing the sand. 'We could talk better.'

'That's all right. I can hear what you say.'

'I come to the beach every week. Every Saturday at this time. I could be here tomorrow too.'

'This is a short holiday for me. I'll be going soon.'

'Let me show you something. We'll have to stand.' He rose, flung his arms wide, took a deep inhalation of sea air and climbed the few paces to the top of the dune where he would be visible to the clothed. 'Come and see,' he said. She joined him.

'For two miles across the dunes,' he waved his hand at the lumpy landscape, 'there are walks for naturists. Lovely places. Really lovely. Would you, I wonder, would you walk with me? Just a short way? We would be quite alone. As though we were the first man and woman ever, walking in the Garden of Eden. It would make the afternoon so beautiful.'

Julia shook her head. 'I really do have to be going now,' she said. She began to dress.

'I could walk along the beach with you. I'll put on my shorts if you like.'

'No, no. You stay here. There's at least an hour or so of sunshine left. You enjoy yourself.'

Julia walked the length of the beach to her car. She did not look for a hotel. She drove straight back to London where her wardrobe would be waiting.

LANGUAGE

Unlike many people, Rita did not write to *The Times* deploring modern standards of English. She preferred to make corrections on the spot.

Sometimes she did this by offering an incentive. This afternoon in the market she negotiated the amendment of 'Brokkoli' on a hand-written sign by agreeing to buy two pounds of the vegetable – or to be precise, flower used as a vegetable. Tom would resent having broccoli for dinner again, she knew. But unfortunately it was misspelt far more often than peas or spring greens or even aubergine, although that, too, was a difficult word.

On other occasions Rita found, as she did with the children, that a certain sharp authority was more effective. Today she decided that 'house clearences' lettered on a junk shop window was intolerable. She went into the shop.

For a moment she stood in the doorway, allowing her eyes to adjust to the gloomy interior. On either side furniture was piled in high, precarious heaps. She could distinguish desks, torn chairs, filing cabinets and Beautility tables. Further away, in the dim recesses of the shop, the individual items merged together, with just a leg discernible here, an upholstered arm protruding there. She stepped forward and discovered, sitting at a desk which stood the right way up, a small dark man.

'Your business cannot hope to succeed,' she announced, her voice booming in the narrow space. 'First impressions count. The impression your shop gives will deter potential customers.' She pointed her finger at the lettering on the window. 'The "E" should be an "A".'

Later that afternoon, when she had finished her shopping and passed the shop a second time, she found the E had been changed to an A. Just as, when she informed her class of noisy fourteen-year-olds that there was to be 'no more of that', there was no more.

When she arrived at the bus station she saw on the wall behind her bold, splashy writing in foreign characters, Arabic maybe or Urdu, and small, disordered scribbles around the glass faces of the timetables, which, although an irritation, caused Rita no real pain. 'Fred was here', 'Mandy loves Greg', 'Joey sucks' were inane, but neither the grammar nor the spelling could be faulted.

On the bus home she passed, as usual, the new industrial estate. Someone had painted an 'I' between the words 'TO' and 'LET' on the boarded up windows.

She left the bus, walked down the main road to the corner, turned into her own road and saw scrawled in black beneath her feet 'cunt'. The word had not been there when she left that morning. 'Shit' was painted on the next flagstone. She scuffed at it with the tip of one brown brogue but it did not even smudge. 'Balls' was the next word she came across, a few yards further on. She accepted this was the kind of thing children wrote on the pavement nowadays. But what had happened to hopscotch? She remembered drawing with white chalk the six squares for hopping and, at the far end, a semicircle which she labelled 'BED'.

The words on the pavement were common currency nowadays; although Rita's mother would have found them deeply offensive. 'Language!' her mother would cry when Rita or her brother Bob said even 'crikey' or 'blimey'. Her mother's voice would fill with outrage. Their grandmother, she said, would have washed out their mouths that instant with carbolic soap. The threat was enough to stop Rita and Bob going as far as their friends with real rude words. Instead they went in for archaic exclamations such as 'Botheration!' or made up their own: 'Slitherkins!' 'Pistoops!' and the somehow more daring 'Oh zags!'.

Rita wheeled her tartan shopping trolley past 'cock' and 'tit'. Remarkable, she thought, how many of these terms were familiar to quite young children. Certainly, in her classroom, sex was the topic on which she knew their vocabulary to be widest, in spite of the fact that it didn't receive the level of attention she insisted they devote to the subjects on the curriculum. She wheeled on. 'Brest' stared up at her from the pavement. She wheeled on again. She reached her house.

Rita let herself into the house with the Yale. The kitchen was already dark. She looked through the french windows. The back garden was a small square of lawn bordered by rhododendrons which, in turn, were surrounded by a high wattle fence. Neither Rita nor Tom used the garden for anything apart from mowing and weeding. She drew the curtains.

She went into the living room where she settled down at the dining table to mark compositions. Why did so many of the children put the 'e' and the 'i' the wrong way round again in 'their'? She circled 'unneccessary' in one effort, wrote in the margin of another 'participal phrase must refer to grammatical subject'.

Tom arrived at twenty to eight – on schedule for his daily journey from London. He awarded Rita the customary homecoming kiss. It was a brief kiss but Rita no longer felt aggrieved by that.

'Had a good day? What's for dinner?' he asked. She told him. 'Broccoli again,' he said with little real enthusiasm. He went upstairs. There he would remove his jacket, his waistcoat and his tie, roll up his sleeves and wash his hands. Possibly he also washed his face, she did not know, never having asked him. Until bedtime, no further kiss would be offered in which, had it been, she might, or might not, have detected the scent of soap.

'How about your day?' she asked, over dinner.

'Trouble with the trains again. All very well them claiming these improvements to commuter lines. No seven fifty-three this morning. No eight o two. I'd have taken my overcoat if I'd known. You know how damp it was this morning. I think I might have caught a cold.'

'For them to claim' would not have jarred the ear in the same way, she thought, but did not say.

After dinner he leaned back on the sofa, she sat upright across the room in a matching easy chair. They watched *News at Ten*. A junior Defence Minister attempted to explain that a bomb might easily be planted in a barracks: 'Anyone could walk in as long as they were carrying a package which did not look suspicious.'

'He means,' said Rita, slowly, in her loud classroom voice, 'anyone could walk in as long as he or she were not carrying a package that did look suspicious.'

'I wanted to hear what else he had to say,' complained Tom.

'An early night for me,' was the next thing from him, while she stayed as always, to complete the *Guardian* crossword.

'You go on up,' she said. 'There's some Lem Sip in the medicine cabinet.'

'What about you?'

'I'll just finish up in the kitchen.'

For once her motive for staying downstairs was not to avoid the bedroom routine – his request and her reluctant compliance. Tonight, her craving to correct had the sharp tingle of sherbert.

Silence upstairs. Tom had settled down swiftly. He might read for a while but he would not come downstairs, would not hear anything if she were quiet. She found black paint in one of the kitchen cupboards, left over from the time Tom had painted the front door, and a brush. She levered the lid off the pot with a screwdriver, stirred the contents, replaced the top lightly and loaded the lot, along with a small torch, into a shopping bag.

Less than half an hour later she cleaned the brush in white spirit and pressed the lid of the tin noiselessly down. She went upstairs and completed the usual preparations for bed. In the bathroom she slid dental floss in and out between her teeth. She washed her face and smoothed cream over her skin. In the bedroom she took off her blouse and skirt and hung them carefully in the wardrobe. She folded her slip and draped it over a chair. She added her underwear to Tom's Y-fronts in the laundry basket. She slipped into her nightie and slid into bed beside Tom, who was asleep and breathing through his mouth. She would not wake him or touch him or even lie close enough to feel his warmth.

In the beginning, more than fifteen years ago, when she was much slimmer and wore flared trousers, she seemed to enter a magnetic field whenever she came close to Tom. Once within range, parts of her body could not be prevented from touching parts of his. If she sat beside him her head would loll onto his shoulder and stay there for long moments. If they were both standing, perhaps having drinks with friends, she would lean towards him and her glass would tilt and spill. Her hands also behaved unexpectedly. The heel of one of them might massage his arm or the rough texture of his cheek. Some of these incidents occurred, regrettably, in public.

Even after marriage, even in the bed in which she was now trying to lie disturbingly still, Tom was embarrassed by the caresses that brought Rita such pleasure. With effort, vast at first, diminishing by slow degrees, she suppressed her body's compulsions. And bit by bit their lovemaking turned into a dry ritual which caused Rita no actual pain, only a lingering, grey regret. Eventually she found other things to do when, in his view, it was time to do that.

In the morning Tom said he had a cold. Not bad enough, he judged, for him to stay in bed but bad enough to keep him at home. Rita made sure that he had a supply of Kleenex and Lem Sip and left for school, approving on the way the neatness with which she had changed 'brest' to 'breast'. Though to be really professional she should make corrections in red as she did in the children's books.

On the way back that afternoon she bought a can of red spray paint in a car accessories shop. At home she found Tom looking better, though serious. He blew his nose and said: 'I don't have a cold. I stayed home so we'd have time this evening. I want to talk to you.'

'Can it wait till I've started dinner? And corrected 4b's grammar?'

'Can't you ever think about anything but correcting grammar?'

'The compositions are always so bad I can only face them if I do so right away.'

'This is important.'

'4b's are the worst of all.'

'I'm seeing someone else.'

'Why do none of the children distinguish between "it's" and "its"? I've told them often enough.'

'I've fallen in love with someone.'

'They sprinkle commas around for absolutely no reason.'

'She wants me to move in with her. I told her I'd tell you today.'

'Restrictive clauses, for instance. There is just no justification.'

'She wants to have children and you never did.'

'Nominative not objective pronoun in a comparison where the verb is understood.'

'I want to marry her. I want a divorce.'

'Imagine putting two "ts" in writing.'

'We can still be friends. You know you've not been interested in sex for years.'

She picked up the bag that held the can of red spray paint and left the living room in silence. She stepped out of the front door and closed it behind her.

She stood on the pavement and pointed the spray can at the low brick wall of their front garden. 'Unclean' she sprayed in bold script and below that 'adulterer'. She moved to the neighbours' wall and sprayed 'fornicator' and 'debauchee'. Next door but one came in for 'concupiscence' and 'whoremonger'. By the third house she completed 'lecher', 'libertine' and 'licentious' before she heard Tom mutter: 'Rita, please. People are looking.'

She turned the spray and stained the white front of his shirt blood red, then turned back and slowly wrote 'carnal knowledge', 'impudicity'.

Had she looked she would indeed have seen many faces peeking from behind twitched curtains, but she was too busy with 'copulation', 'coition', 'clitoris', 'testicles' and 'fuck'.

By the time someone called the police the street boasted red descriptions of every aspect of straight sex along with some more arcane terms such as 'fellatio', 'cunnilingus' and 'onanism'.

'It's quite all right,' she said to the young, pink faced WPC. 'The can is, in any case, almost empty.'

Rita sat in the back of the police car as she was told to do. A broad shouldered constable sat beside her. The young WPC drove.

At the police station Rita sat on a wooden bench and answered questions. The policeman typed his version of what she said on an old manual Remington.

He finished typing, took the paper from the machine and gave it to her. She examined the statement.

'Too many passive verbs,' she said. 'Very common nowadays and makes for flabby, colourless prose. I said I was "loath" not "loathe". Occurrence with an "e" not an "a". When a quotation is followed by an attributive phrase, the comma is placed within the quotation marks. In all other respects I agree it is an entirely accurate record of the event.'

THE RIGHT TO WORK

I haven't had a job for a year now. I don't mean I'm unemployed, God forbid. I go to work each day. I have an office to myself. I send minutes laid out in the proper style. I even have a job title – Special Projects Officer – but I have no work. Not since they abolished my real job. They couldn't sack me, though. I'd done nothing wrong.

At first it was a bit of a blow. Having your real job abolished must mean there was no real job in the first place. Or they didn't think there was. Also it was hard to know what to say to Anne – that's my wife – when she asked each evening 'How was your day?' It wasn't enough for her, after spending the day on her own, hoovering, shopping and running the washing machine, so she said, for me to retell a couple of jokes from the *Telegraph* diary.

The problem was that there were no special projects. I drew this to the attention of Mellowes, my line manager, at an early stage and he had made vague noises about something being in the pipeline.

I'm a civil servant; not very senior, but I get by. And even though I have no real job, I believe that life is what you make of it. Besides, it would be a criminal waste of taxpayers' money if I did nothing. We're not all as bad as we're painted.

So I spent my first month as Special Projects Officer looking for work. I read all through the papers dropped into my in-tray marked 'for information only'. I spotted a critical piece about my department in the *Economist* and drafted a letter to the editor for Mellowes to send but he didn't use it. One morning I received a report on the terms of reference for the Service-wide performance review and wrote a minute to its author stressing the need to define the concept of work.

When I told Anne this she said, somewhat tartly, 'if I redefined the concept of dirt I could stop hoovering the place.'

She doesn't have a job, of course, so she doesn't understand that things are different when you do them for a living.

Next, I studied the staff handbook. I read about the duties of and constraints on employees. I read summaries of the *Health and Safety at Work etc. Act* and went on to other employment and trade union legislation. I absorbed chapter and verse of nationally-negotiated settlements. Then I began on custom and practice – a fascinating subject, because so much depends on precedent rather than formal agreements. Put simply, if it becomes the *custom* or the *practice* of a group of workers to do a job in a certain way and management makes no objection, then that method of working can be cited as a precedent in disputes.

I've never been a trade union man myself, never saw the point, but in terms of research and analysis I found the field a fascinating one. I looked up the name of my shop steward – Chris Pike – in a recent union bulletin, wrote to him for further information and he invited me up to the Branch Office. I was pleasantly surprised at his general attitude. No chip on his shoulder. A genuine man, I would say, a man of principle. He introduced me to the Branch Secretary, Forbes, who I found less congenial, more prone to rhetoric, though at his level I daresay it was expected of him.

It was Pike who put me onto the Department's Legal Section. I went along there one afternoon and stuck my head round the door; saw two men in the sort of office you'd expect of solicitors – box files in neat rows and shelf upon shelf of law reports.

I announced myself. 'Illingsworth,' I said, 'Special Projects. Looking into custom and practice. Thought you might be able to help with a few snippets of case law.'

'Harrington,' said the smaller, dark one. 'Give us an idea where you want to begin.' 'Lewis,' the other one rose to his feet and extended his hand. 'Pre- or post- Fulton?'

We spent a most agreeable couple of hours, the three of us. Harrington and Lewis both said they found it a pleasant change from their usual routine. 'Drop in any time,' said Lewis as I rose to go. I looked in on them fairly frequently after that.

Between whiles I worked hard. I read and made notes. As an exercise and to test my familiarity with the material, I drafted a summary of disputes procedures, both national and local, confining myself to a single sheet of A4. Most succinct. When I finished I took the lift down to the typing pool. 'Mrs Carter,' I said to the supervisor, 'by tomorrow, please. Double-spaced, with side heads in caps,' then took the lift up again.

Next morning I checked the typing for errors and sent it back for correction. After lunch I reread and filed the summary. I did not plan to submit it to anyone. The pursuit of excellence was sufficient unto itself.

But mid-way through the afternoon the door opened. Pike came in. 'Can you spare a moment?' I nodded. He sat in the chair in front of my desk. 'Any idea where I could lay my hands on an idiot's guide to disputes?' he asked. 'It's for the new stewards' training day.' So I gave him a copy of my summary.

After he left it occurred to me that Harrington and Lewis might also find my effort useful, so I took them a copy.

Within days my summary was in demand throughout the Department. I wrote a similar piece entitled 'The Grievance Procedure, Step by Step' which also went down well. I read more widely and, as news of my expertise spread, people began to seek me out for a ruling on a specific industrial relations issue or for an historical precedent. It was all at my fingertips and I was only too pleased to be of some assistance, from whatever quarter the request came. I was straight with all of them, mind you, made it quite clear I had no axe to grind.

Then I branched out into a new area. Once again it was Pike's idea. I set out to clarify my own circumstances vis-à-vis employment rights. I examined my contract and pointed out a minor discrepancy in it to Personnel. They were most amenable and forwarded a corrected contract without delay. By now they too knew they could call on me.

I checked my job description. It was vague in the extreme. 'To undertake Special Projects,' it read. Quite a come-down from the two-page list of duties required of me when I had a real job. A thought struck me. I checked with Pike and found I was correct: according to custom and practice my job description formed a part of my contract. Had I known that the previous year, I could have made a good case to contest the abolition of my old job.

Each evening I reported to Anne, keeping it light for the most part. 'But are you actually getting anywhere?' she asked. 'What about promotion? It sounds such a dead end job.'

It was a little irritating of her. And unjust. I did, after all, earn a decent living. I planned to tell her so, but left it for tonight. In any case, she was absorbed in her patchwork.

She has rather a thing about patchwork. She borrows books on it from the local library and copies out old patterns. While I cannot see the attraction, at least it keeps her busy in the evenings.

Next morning I found a note on my desk. 'See me. 9.30. Mellowes,' I read.

Bit of a shock after all this time, to be summoned to my line manager's office. When I went in he was sitting at his desk with a file open in front of him. He waited for me to take a chair. 'Well, Frank,' he said. He always uses my first name, although he is several years my junior. He looked at the file. 'You joined us from Central Records, I see. Another victim of the cuts.' I didn't reply. It was all in the file.

'Well, Frank,' he said again. 'You've been with us, now, near on a year.'

'Almost to the day.'

'Right. Well. I won't beat about the bush. There's been a complaint.'

'Complaint? About what?'

He looked straight at me. 'I assume you know the state of play in the admin assistants'dispute?'

'No,' I said with interest. And surprise. The admin assistants reported to Personnel, not to Mellowes.

'Deadlock. Complete stalemate.'

'That's unfortunate. I'd heard on the grapevine it was nearly settled.'

'Frank, I'll come to the point. Did you let the management negotiating team know they could use bonus payments as a bargaining tool?'

'I did indeed. They were most grateful.'

'Did you tell the trade union side about an obscure precedent which would allow for their claim to the bonus?'

I thought for a moment. There was no point in denying the truth. 'Correct again,' I said.

'Did you then suggest to the management team that, although the administrative assistants were arguing for parity with the statistical clerks, reference should be made to similar groups in the private sector?'

'That's right.'

'And point out to the union that the comparable grade in local government already had higher pay and a thirty-five hour week?'

'Yes.'

'It has to stop. You've had ample time to get your feet under the table by now and one or two things have come up which I'd like you to pursue. Urgent stuff.' He pushed two thick buff folders across his desk. 'Cast your eyes over these. Get through as much as you can this afternoon. By five p.m. I'll expect results.'

I took the folders to my office. I was more than a little put out. I had planned to spend the day analysing the knock-on effects for the statistical clerks of a three per cent increase in the admin assistants' salaries. I sighed, opened the first folder and flipped through it.

It contained instructions on different sheets of paper in different handwriting. 'Check on remaining supplies of Form NLZ/897246 with Regional Offices and issue replacement Form NLZ/897247 as appropriate,' read the first one. 'Send standard acknowledgment to enclosed letters,' read the second. I slammed the file shut and got on the blower right away. 'Pike,' I said to my shop steward, 'I'd like your advice,' and explained what had happened.

He was over like a shot. He opened the file. 'It's the admin assistants' work all right,' he announced. 'Held up on account of their work to rule. If you were to go ahead it would be strikebreaking. Don't touch it with a bargepole.'

I returned the folders to Mellowes during the lunch hour with a note explaining that union instructions prevented my undertaking the work. A good thing I was free of it, as both sides in the dispute applied to me for further information in the course of the afternoon. As Mellowes said, negotiations had reached a tricky stage. The management rep told me he'd even heard whispers of sympathetic action among the statistical clerks.

Next morning when I arrived there were two new buff folders on my desk. I took a look inside: computer printouts of columns of figures. I dialled the Branch Office extension. Pike, as I expected, confirmed that this was work which was normally done by the statistical clerks. It stood to reason that it must be someone's job; anything that Mellowes gave me was bound to be.

During the next two days I advised on industrial relations problems in catering, computers and property services and sent back three more folders of work to my line manager. On the Friday Pike dropped in to see me.

'Mellowes is gunning for you,' he said as he sat down. 'Hope you won't take this the wrong way; I've asked Forbes to issue you a formal warning of expulsion from the union if you touch work which is in anyone else's job description. It's for your protection, so that you have the union behind you if Mellowes kicks up a stink. Oh, and we're backdating the warning to cover the stuff you returned to him last week.'

My weekend began very pleasantly. I did a few odds and ends in the garden on Saturday, played a round of golf on Sunday morning. But Anne was late serving Sunday lunch. She apologised of course; I gathered she'd been talking quilts with a fellow enthusiast and had forgotten the time. The fact remained that the beef was overcooked and some of the potatoes were burned. I didn't say anything, just put the bits I couldn't eat on the side of my plate.

Then, in the afternoon, I came in from the garden and found her in an armchair, engrossed in a thick, glossy-looking book.

'Something new from the library?' I asked, taking an interest. When she didn't reply I crossed the room, stood with one hand on the back of her chair and watched her turn pages of colour plates of patchwork quilts.

'That library does you proud,' I said. 'Ordering special books.'

She turned and looked at me. 'It's not from the library. I bought it.'

I really felt she had gone too far; the book must have cost a small fortune.

'How much did you pay for it? As a matter of interest.'

'I bought it with my own money.'

She always does this – assumes that the money is hers when she saves something out of the housekeeping. I earned it in the first place, so strictly speaking it's still mine; but you learn not to say some things in marriage.

Monday morning. As usual we had breakfast in the conservatory. I cast my eye over the front page of the *Telegraph* while Anne poured the coffee. I looked at my watch; 'Is there more toast?' I asked. 'I've time for another slice.' But Anne said 'Frank, there's something about you in the paper. Oh dear.'

'About me?' I took her *Daily Mail*. 'A Year's Pay for Nothing,' read the headline. There must have been a leak. I read the rest of the story; the gist of it was I had idled away a year on full pay and what was the Government going to do about it? There was also a quote from Forbes; he praised the stand I had taken in the face of management victimisation and stressed my right to real work. I put down the *Mail*, opened *the Telegraph* and found the same tale, though told in less lurid terms.

I folded the paper and looked at Anne. 'Well!' I said, 'that should ruffle a few feathers,' but she didn't seem the least impressed.

'How did you get yourself into this mess?' she asked. 'Can't you just do the work you're paid for?'

'That's the nub. I am the Special Projects Officer. Mellowes has assigned me to the duties of the administrative assistants, then to those of the statistical clerks. It's iniquitous. And divisive. I wasn't expecting the press to get hold of it, mind you; but it may be no bad thing.'

'I would have thought your work was whatever Mellowes told you to do.'

As I've said, she doesn't understand these things.

I received rather more satisfactory reactions at work. I walked in the front door of the Department and the receptionist said 'Good morning, Mr Illingsworth,' which she never normally did. In the lift a man I hadn't come across before spoke to me. 'Illingsworth, isn't it?' he asked. 'You've certainly caused a stir.'

I hurried out of the lift, along the corridor and opened the door to my office. No buff folders on the desk today. Instead there was a solitary red one. I crossed the room and picked it up, still wearing my coat. The folder was marked 'priority'. I opened it. An opposition MP had tabled a question in parliament. About me. I took off my coat quickly and tossed it on the chair in front of my desk. I sat down and read further. The Minister was to answer the question this afternoon. Mellowes had drafted a reply for him to read out. A note from Mellowes instructed me to cast my eye over the draft, pronto, for inaccuracies. This, being in the nature of a special project, I did.

It would have been an education to have been in the House when the Minister spoke. But I received another note from Mellowes; it said I was not to leave the office; I was not to answer the phone; above all I was not to speak to the press.

I drafted a statement for the trade union, detailing the nature of their support for me and hinting at a readiness to take further action were the matter not resolved in days. I called Pike and read it to him. He was delighted, said he would mark it for immediate release to the newspapers under the Branch Secretary's name.

I then drafted a statement for the management side and sent it by hand to Mellowes who was sufficiently impressed by this initiative to pop his head around the door an hour later with a look of something less than mistrust.

I reviewed the position. I was employed by the civil service to carry out special projects. Hitherto management had identified no special projects. On the other hand no one else did the work I had been doing over the past year. Therefore it could be classified as a special project – one for which there was constant demand. My records were frequently consulted, my opinion often sought. I was indispensable.

After these reflections I formulated my demands. My bottom line was to retain the status quo. So often the parties to disputes make the mistake of not being crystal-clear about the bottom line. I scratched my head. I checked a couple of precedents in my files. I thought for a while. I added a number of subsidiary claims. I varied the audacity of these to ensure the change of pace and tone so essential to a good negotiating table.

I imagined the scene: Mellowes at one end of the table, Forbes at the other. I would send in a note addressed to Mellowes. He would read it, nod and announce that he was ready to make a concession. Forbes would request an adjournment. I would be waiting for him outside the room and would suggest that he too withdraw a minor claim; then add a new demand. The final settlement, as with the various disputes to which the Department seemed ever more prone, would be in my gift and mine alone.

I finished my list of demands and took it to the Branch Office, where I received something of a hero's welcome. Pike shook my hand; Forbes slapped me on the back. He would fight my case to the bitter end, he vowed.

Over dinner that evening I told Anne everything that had happened. Told it rather well, I thought. 'So you see,' I concluded, 'I'm sure I can put the wind up Mellowes.' She looked at me across the dining table, frowned and said, 'I don't see the point.'

I sighed. I explained again: about my job description, custom and practice and my right to do the work for which I was employed. She said, 'I still don't see the point. By the way I'm taking on homeworkers.'

This rather threw me. I put down my knife and fork and said, 'You keep the place beautifully.'

'Homeworkers. Not somebody to clean. People who work at home. For me.'

'You mean someone to take in the ironing? Or the laundry? Is that the cheapest way?'

'I'd be employing women for sewing. Quilting to my designs.'

'Quilting? Whatever for? The house is full of your little efforts.'

'So I'll have more time for designing. For marketing.'

'What on earth are you talking about Anne? I haven't been in the least difficult about your doing all that sewing. Even though it does seem to have taken over the house a bit.'

'I've been selling patchwork for some time now,' she went on. 'I thought I'd wait until I made a go of it before I told you. Now I've more orders than I can handle. I'm ready to expand.'

'Orders? Expand? But you don't need to work. Not for a living.'

'Well I am.'

'Look,' I said. 'It's tough out there in the real world. Competition. Cut and thrust. Take my situation; you'd never be able to handle that, would you? You ought to think again.'

But she said, 'If you've finished your cottage pie, I'll fetch the pudding,' and rose to her feet. I sat there with my elbows on the table. Fancy hitting me with this. After the day I'd had at work. You'd almost think she did it on purpose.

DISPLACEMENT ACTIVITY

Don had backaches and headaches. He suffered from bouts of indigestion. He could no longer keep his eyes open to watch any one of the Thrill-a-Minute videos which, until quite recently, would have kept him on the edge of his seat. Tonight he had been immersed in scenes of Mafia violence and found himself the next moment slumped in the Chesterfield staring at silver snow on the screen. The film was over.

He rubbed his eyes, rose slowly and went into the bedroom. He undressed, but could not bother to do so in the proper order, to remove his socks before stepping out of trousers and boxer shorts. Anyway Amanda was dead to the world.

He slipped in beside her and crunched on the dusty taste of a Rennie. He lay on his back for a few moments as he always did, then turned onto his right side, arranging himself as if for sleep. It was too much to hope for. His short doze in the living room had been long enough to keep him awake now. With weary patience he watched the room's familiar objects assume slow, grey shapes. Amanda rolled over taking most of the duvet with her; it was easier to let her have more than her fair share. He sighed, closed his eyes and drifted finally into uneasy sleep.

In the morning he woke to find Amanda already up and well on the way with preparations for her day, to judge by the clattering coming from the kitchen.

The bedroom door opened and she rushed in. 'Want anything ironed?' she asked and dumped a mug on the bedside table with such vigour that steaming coffee splashed in Don's direction. She flung the wardrobe open, riffled the line of clothes, selected a blouse, waved it at him, added, '. . . while I'm doing this,' and rushed out again.

Don sat up and sipped his coffee. Amanda filled the flat with so much energy it hurt: humming, calling out snatches of news from the radio, crunching toast at a painful volume. He pushed the duvet aside and rose to his feet.

In the bathroom he peered in the mirror at the creases on his forehead; surely they were deeper than they had been yesterday. He probed the puffy white bags under his eyes with a tentative finger. Oh well. Better make a start on shaving. 'You nearly ready yet?' called Amanda. Did she have to shout at him?

By the time he finished in the bathroom she was fully dressed in a bright yellow suit with padded shoulders. Her hair was a blonde cloud. She smiled cheerily. To look at her made Don want to go back to bed. 'Tell me the truth,' he said. 'Do you think my eyes are sinking?'

That evening Don arrived at Amanda's flat just before eight. 'Hi,' she said as she let him in. 'I'm only just back myself. Had a rush job on.' He didn't reply, but made straight for the Chesterfield. She stood in the living room doorway and frowned at him. 'You should have had an early night,' she commented. 'You don't have to come round if you're not up to it. Did you pick up the video?'

'I would have. I was whacked.'

She shrugged. 'I'm going to change,' and went into the

bedroom; so he didn't find out what she was wearing underneath. What Amanda was wearing underneath had once been a matter of passionate interest to Don.

After a moment he rose slowly, poured himself a whisky, returned to the Chesterfield and took a dismal sip. Amanda came back wearing a tee-shirt and black leggings, made herself a large gin and tonic, sat down and drank. They used to share a bottle of wine, Don reflected. Quite good wine, which he used to select carefully on the way to her place.

'You could have tried,' she grumbled. 'The reviews say *Wall Street*'s well worth watching.'

'I didn't know I was going to feel so knocked out. Perhaps I ought to see a doctor.'

'What do you want to do now? It's too late to get anything else.'

'Nothing. Watch television. I had a hard day. And I didn't get a lot of sleep last night.'

'You only come here to crash out.' Amanda inspected her drink. To do this she unwrapped her legs from each other, bent her right knee briefly and peered into the empty glass. In one movement she was on her feet and en route for the drinks table. She paused at the mantelpiece to move a small cactus a couple of inches to the left.

'I'm tired. I've a headache. Do you think I have M.E?' asked Don.

Amanda filled her glass and spun round to face him. 'Displacement activity,' she said and headed back to the mantelpiece where she swapped a silver-framed photograph for a white porcelain horse. 'That's what your tiredness is,' she pronounced over her shoulder. 'And your headaches. And your indigestion. No one can be tired all the time. You must really want to be doing something else but you won't let yourself admit it.' She turned to the mantelpiece. 'They look better like that don't they?'

Don, knowing he should say something, managed 'The horse is crooked.'

'Is that better?' Amanda bounced to attend to it. 'Like this? This? Or should I put them back where they were?'

'Do you think you could sit down? There was something I wanted to say.' His eyelids were beginning to droop. 'It's too much.'

'You could have another drink.' Amanda returned to her chair. 'You could try to guess what I'm wearing.'

'You said you had an early start tomorrow. And my first meeting is at eight thirty.'

Amanda stood up again, crossed the room, took a blue bowl of chrysanths from the coffee table and carried them across the room to the dresser.

'It's all this toing and froing,' said Don. 'It takes it out of me. And I worry in case someone needs to ring me.'

'You've put this number on your answerphone.'

'Amanda,' said Don, making a last ditch attempt. 'This stuff about your place or mine is all very well. But it's been going on for two years.'

'No one's forcing you. And I do come to your place.' Amanda looked at a picture on the wall. 'One of us must have knocked that. It's not straight.'

'I just think we should live together.'

'Not at yours. Your cooker's electric.'

'Buy a place. Something we both like.'

'Don't you like this flat? You said you did.'

'You know I do. But it's not big enough.'

'You stay over often enough.'

'That's different. There's nowhere for my clothes. We're always on top of each other.'

'If you say so.' Amanda uncoiled her legs again and stood up. 'Do you think the speakers would give a better quality of sound if I moved them further apart?'

It was Don who made the effort; he bought the local paper and looked at ads for houses; he phoned estate agents and asked for lists of properties. 'Highgate,' he said to Amanda. 'What do you reckon? It's almost like being in the country. Lots of trees. And the schools are good.'

'Schools,' Amanda said to Don, 'are places to send children. I do not have any children.'

'It's only what they all said. Shows it's a good area.'

Don even gave up his Saturday. He set out at ten; he viewed as many houses as possible, trudged across miles of fitted carpet and sanded floors, exchanged weary smiles with anxious vendors. By the time he arrived at Amanda's he was ready to drop.

'Oh, good,' she said, when she saw him. 'You're just in time to give me a hand.'

He stopped in the living room doorway and looked, appalled, at the room. The Chesterfield, onto which he was ready to drop, was no longer at its usual, comfortable angle to the television. It stood in the middle of the room, apparently on its way somewhere. The television was unplugged. The drinks were heaped in Amanda's chair. 'What on earth have you been doing?' he demanded. 'There's nowhere to sit.'

'The least you could do is take the other end of the Chesterfield,' Amanda said crossly. He did. 'It's going over there, I think,' she went on. 'Where the drinks table is. The table is coming out of the alcove and the armchair is going in. Then there's the television.'

'You can't move the television!'

'It's all right. I bought an extension lead for the aerial point. We could even watch it in bed.'

'Why?' asked Don, stopping to draw breath. 'Why are you doing this? We'll only have to go through it all again when we move.' The thought filled him with exhaustion.

'I forgot,' said Amanda, perching on the arm of the stranded chair. 'You don't know about this. Look.' She pointed to a huge mirror with an ornate surround which was leaning against the wall. 'I picked it up at Camden Lock.'

'You can't have. It must weigh a ton.'

'If I managed to get it home with the help of a cabbie we must be able to move it between the two of us. Mind the plasterwork, though.' Amanda took one end of the mirror.

'Where?' asked Don.

'Over the fireplace. So I can see if it looks okay. Then I'll put in rawlplugs and hang it properly.'

'It'll be a fixture with rawlplugs. What's the point when you won't be here?'

'I've bought it,' said Amanda, 'and I want to see it up.'

The following Saturday she agreed, at least, to go with him but then all she did was pick holes: 'Carpet's frayed,' she said, after inspecting an apparently immaculate place in Muswell Hill; 'Too far from the shops,' of a modern luxury development on the prestigious fringes of Hampstead Heath; and of the one he'd had real hopes for, a newly-converted maisonette over towards Crouch End – 'original features all been taken out. Pity. And look at those trees. I'm sure they're the sort that drop sticky stuff on the top of the car.'

Their last port of call was a large, unmodernised house. Amanda's face brightened as soon as they were inside. 'Potential,' she said, 'definite potential. Nice high ceilings. Where's that damp coming from?'

Don raised his head while his heart sank. They could have it done professionally, he supposed, wearily imagining a pile of builders' estimates.

The house was full of little flights of steps where he least expected them. There were many dark, stained rooms. 'I would have had it done,' said the owner, a small, pale woman, 'but I'm selling up to go and live with my sister and it didn't seem worth it.'

'Much better not.' Amanda confronted, with relish, the unrenovated kitchen. 'They do such awful things.'

Outside the kitchen were brambles and thistles as far as the eye could see. 'Hundred foot garden,' said the woman and Amanda set off to verify this while Don and the woman waited. If Amanda would only get it over with, thought Don.

It was late in the evening when Don and Amanda returned to Amanda's flat. Don lowered himself onto the Chesterfield. Amanda went into the kitchen and returned with two packets of crisps. 'Catch,' she challenged and tossed one of them in his direction. She dumped herself on the Chesterfield beside him and ripped open her own packet, noisily. 'That was quite a place,' she enthused. 'Imagine the huge room at the front painted a sort of duck-egg blue. A golden sunshine yellow would suit the bathroom. We'll need to put in a new suite.' She twisted her legs up under her, crunched a crisp, ran a hand through her hair and turned towards him. 'The back faces south, so it will be in full sun,' she went on. 'We could build on a garden room.' She paused. 'Did you see the varnish in the kitchen though? And layers of gloss on those lovely shutters. It'll take us forever to strip them right down. What shall we do tonight? Shall we go out?'

Don said, 'I'm exhausted. You know crisps give me indigestion. And why can't you leave things the way they are?'

'Don't be silly. We couldn't live there with it in that state.'

'That seems to be exactly what you are planning to do.'

'Only till we get it straight.'

'It's crazy. When we could have the maisonette for the same price. Amanda I'm not twenty years old. I'm not even thirty and nor are you. Why can't you settle down?'

'You know what?' said Amanda. 'I think this room was better the way it was before. Don't you?'

'Yes.'

'Even with the mirror? Could you give me a hand?'

'For God's sake, Amanda. We'll be up half the night.'

'So what? It's Sunday tomorrow. You can have a nice lie in.'

'Amanda, I haven't been sleeping well.'

'You don't come here to go to sleep. You didn't used to.'

'It's no good talking when you're like this. I'm going to bed.'

'No you're not.'

'Who's stopping me?'

'I am. I don't want you to go to bed. It's my bed. And I'm sick and tired of it.'

'You mean you don't want me to stay? You want me to go? You don't want me to sleep here?'

'I don't want anyone to go to sleep. Anywhere. It's half-past nine on a Saturday evening for Christ's sake. If I had any children to send to those good schools in Highgate, even they wouldn't be asleep by now.'

'If that's how you feel, I'll go to my own flat.'

'Fine by me. The last thing I want to do is to share a place with a couch potato. You're getting a paunch, did you know that?'

Don's flat, after all those nights at Amanda's, was not the most welcoming place in the world. He shivered; he put the central heating on 'constant'; he went round the corner for a bottle of whisky. He returned and sat on his cold, leather sofa flicking channels.

He did not call Amanda for a week. When he did her answerphone answered. Don did not have backache that night. He did not have a headache although he listened to his old albums at full volume. He did not have indigestion although he ate ready salted crisps with his whisky. Nor was he in the least tired until well after midnight.

The next night he remembered to pick up a video on the way back from work. He sat upright on the sofa and watched the whole film. Then, the following night, half-way through a political thriller, he became so restless that he rewound the tape and took it back to the shop; but the shop was closed. The third night he went straight from work to a wine bar.

In the wine bar he bought drinks for two young women. He chatted to them all evening, then went home and fell asleep. The following evening he went to a different wine bar and bought drinks for two different young women. Most nights, at some point, he thought about phoning Amanda but he always managed, at the last moment, to replace the receiver before her answerphone answered. He managed to do other things too; on Saturdays he went to the gym to lift weights. On Sunday he played squash and on weekday mornings he jogged for twenty minutes before work. No time for insomnia, backaches, headaches, indigestion or general lethargy. He felt a lot better. On the evidence of his bathroom mirror, he looked better too.

So much better, in fact, that he could no longer resist the urge to go and see Amanda.

He rang the bell to her flat. The door opened and there she stood. She was wearing a huge orange tee shirt and black leggings and looked exactly as she always looked. But the door, he realised, as the light from inside fell on it, was not black as before, but bright pink.

'Come in,' she said. 'You're just in time to give me a hand.' He followed her, but stopped in the living room doorway and looked at the room. The fitted carpet was gone. The floorboards were sanded. The walls were no longer white, but pale green. The ornate mirror was firmly fixed on the wall opposite the fireplace. There were new shelves in the alcove where the drinks table once stood. The porcelain horse, the cactus, the blue bowl and the drinks were on the shelves. The television was on the drinks table. The armchair in which Amanda used to sit had turned green too. And the Chesterfield, which stood, as Don had last seen it, in the middle of the room, waiting to go somewhere, was now plumply buttoned in the most florid of Sanderson prints.

'You didn't call,' said Amanda. 'I thought you didn't want to see me. I had to have something to do.'

'Displacement activity,' said Don. 'You said you didn't want to sleep with me.' He paused. 'Would you like to go out for a drink?'

'I can't leave the Chesterfield like this' Amanda complained.

'I've brought some wine,' said Don. 'The Chesterfield seems fine where it is. We could listen to music instead. What are you wearing under that?'

EXPOSED

'You're different from the women I've met so far,' said Ray. 'You have something special about you.'

Gillian looked at his round pink cheeks, then into his little blue eyes. 'Really?' she asked. 'What exactly?'

'That wasn't a line.' He reached across the table and took her hand, which was a nuisance; he would notice if she tried to look at her watch.

'Anybody coming anywhere near you would feel it. I did immediately.' She toyed with her empty glass. He paused, said, 'You're ready for another drink,' and clicked thumb and fingers of his free hand at a waiter, who showed no sign of feeling anything untoward when he approached Gillian. His hands, transferring glasses from tray to table, did not tremble. He did not even smile at her.

Gillian offered Ray a pack of Marlboro Lights; he released her hand, took one and lit her cigarette, then his. She checked her watch quickly. Nine-fifty. She could make a move in about twenty minutes. In the meantime she was stiff from sitting still; she crossed one knee over the other.

'You have beautiful legs,' Ray tried, but one of the other men had already told her that.

She leant her elbows on the table, clasped her hands lightly and rested her chin on them. She knew this pose showed her slim fingers to advantage. Ray reclaimed her left hand and said, 'What star sign are you? No, let me guess.' He tilted his head to one side, then straightened it again. 'Libra,' he said firmly. 'Artistically inclined, outgoing, a lover of beautiful things.'

'Sagittarius,' Gillian corrected.

'Of course. The Archer. Friendly. Easygoing.' He smiled. 'You like animals. Enjoy the outdoor life. And sports.'

He launched into details of the sporting activities in which he thought she took part. She understood that he was imagining her in a swimsuit with sleek hair at the local pool or in a short, white dress on a tennis court.

'I should be going,' she said, hoping that the time was a convincing one by now. 'You said you lived near Vauxhall, didn't you? Victoria line. I'm on the Northern.'

Her trick was to establish during the early part of the evening roughly where the man lived; then to announce a destination for herself to which he could not suggest accompanying her without seeming over keen.

Only with the first man had she got this wrong. What was his name again? Checked shirt, windcheater with a black zip, brown hair, thinning slightly. Freelance science writer. Had a Hornby OO-gauge railway in his attic. Dennis, that was it. With Dennis she made the mistake of saying where she lived before he did.

'It'll be no trouble at all to see you to your door,' he had lied. To avoid the trouble she had been obliged to invent a friend, a suicidal woman friend with whom she was staying that night. The friend lived at the end of the Piccadilly Line so Dennis had insisted on escorting Gillian to Covent Garden when Leicester Square would have been easier for her.

Tonight she had no problem with Ray. They parted at the corner of St Martin's Lane and Gillian made her way home on her own. She left the Tube at Chalk Farm and walked – it was only a few hundred yards. Several paces from her flat she took her keys from her jacket pocket; she kept her keys in her pocket rather than her bag in case of mugging. She unlocked the Chubb. Also the Yale. There were locks on all the windows of the flat too. Gillian had long ago learned to look after herself.

Inside, in the warm living room, with a glass of chilled dry wine to drink and Mozart to listen to on the CD, she was far from the tiredness she had claimed earlier. She was never tired till past midnight. She played back the messages on her answerphone and jotted down the numbers and names of the men who had called: Tony, Ali, Geoff, and Junior.

This time of the night was the best. She relaxed, as satisfied as if she had chaired a difficult meeting through to its triumphant conclusion or been acclaimed at Board level for the fresh approach of her latest report.

She had, after all, done her homework as thoroughly – if anything more thoroughly – than she would have in order to realise either of those goals.

Her preparations had taken six weeks. Before she began them she prepared a timetable. It read:

Week One: Join health club. Begin exercises to increase general fitness, start gentle swimming. Twenty minutes on sun bed (repeat each week). Walk up escalator on way to work. Book course of cosmetic dentistry.

Week Two: Appointment with hairdresser for new style (query highlights). Tackle programme of hair care. Seek advice from health club on exercise routine (to concentrate on stomach and hips). Swim ten lengths twice a week. Walk for fifteen minutes each lunch hour.

Week Three: Facial. Select new skin-care products. Continue exercise programme, increasing swimming to twenty lengths, walking to twenty minutes.

Week Four: Visit image consultant for advice on colours and colour co-ordination. Two-hour workout with weights. Place ad in *New Statesman*.

Week Five: Manicure. Select new make-up and experiment with it. Step up exercise routine (possibly include brisk country walk?). Choose and join executive dating agency.

Week Six: Buy new clothes – to fit new figure – and accessories to transform office clothes into outfit suitable for evening – e.g. scarves, belts, bracelets, chokers.

Then she followed the timetable.

Everything went according to plan. So many men answered her ad she hadn't replied to all of them yet; and the dating agency supplied a steady stream of potential partners.

Gillian arranged to meet her first date in Leicester Square. She felt conspicuous standing on her own; crowds of young people drifted past. A man in rags asked her for the price of a cup of tea. She wondered whether she would find enough to discuss with a stranger to fill the evening. The clock on the Swiss Centre began to whirr and clang. Surely the man – Dennis – wouldn't turn up late?

She needn't have wondered. Dennis arrived just before the clock chimed the hour. And she hardly had to say a word the whole evening. Not on that date, nor on the ones that followed.

Gillian took a sip of wine, put the glass down on the table in front of her on top of the brochure from the dating agency, slipped off her shoes and curled her feet up under her on the sofa. Her preparations had paid off. Each man took time to compliment her hair, her face, her clothes, her figure; he told her a great deal about herself. When he finished he told her about himself. She thought about the men she had met. Martin, tall with a roll-necked sweater under a grey suit, played war games; John, slightly paunchy with a beard, was into steam trains – he took photos of them; Julian, fair, well-dressed, with crooked teeth, divorced, spent Saturdays with his children and would expect her to do so too if they suited each other; Lewis, in three-piece suit and striped shirt, supported the reintroduction of corporal punishment in schools; Gerald, a mild, bushy-haired man, described with passionate precision the arrangement of the plants in his garden. Only one thing these men had in common – they were sure they wanted to see Gillian again.

Her efforts were, therefore, a success, though not, she had to admit, of the kind promised by the dating agency. She moved her glass, picked up the brochure and leafed through it, studying pictures of happy couples. They came in all shapes and sizes; and all of them claimed to have become permanent partners. But did such relationships really exist, Gillian wondered. If they did, did she want to be part of one? And if the answer was yes, would such a thing happen?

She shook her head and looked at her watch. Twelve midnight. She switched off the CD player, went into the bedroom, checked that her black dress, red jacket and red shoes were spotless for the morning: tucked a red and gold scarf and a couple of gilt bracelets into her bag to wear in the evening and went to bed.

She arrived at work at a quarter to nine and went straight to the studio. 'Your roughs look really good, Charles,' she told the graphic designer. 'The layout you came up with worked out beautifully. Just one small thing. The company name could have a little more prominence. Perhaps a different type face? More white space around it? You'll be the best judge of that. Could you carry the idea through on the headed notepaper? And the business cards? The point-of-sale material? The presentation to Purdy and Roy is at three so you'll need to get cracking.'

Next she went to David's office. 'You've done splendidly,' she said. 'Nice, crisp, clean copy. Purdy and Roy should be pleased with your draft for their Annual Report. I particularly like your ideas for the sub-heads.' A pleased smile spread across David's face. 'One or two minor points,' Gillian went on. 'You could cut this paragraph without losing any of the impact. Perhaps make more of the one before. The section at the back – these three pages – could go here, right after the statement from the Chairman. And in the point-of-sale material just a headline as opposed to the two sentences you have now? I'll leave you to liaise with Charles on that. Can you make sure you both have something to show me by lunchtime? So I can run through it before the presentation.'

Gillian retired to her own office where she prepared her flip charts. At eleven she asked Janice, her PA, to set up the flip charts in the conference room. At twelve she asked her to fetch a salad from the local wholefood bar. At one she ran through her presentation. At two she called Charles and David, went over their revised efforts and made one or two last-minute amendments. By two forty-five her confidence was complete; nothing could stop her now.

The phone on her desk buzzed; Gillian picked it up. 'Mr Purdy and Mr Roy are in reception,' said Janice. Gillian replied, 'Show them into the conference room.'

Gillian and her team reached the conference room at the same time as the clients. 'Mr Purdy. Mr Roy,' Gillian shook hands briskly. 'Coffee? Tea? Do have a seat.' Janice took their orders while Gillian studied the two men. Purdy, she judged, would try to rile her. But she suspected he was all front. Roy looked much more solid – the kind of man who would sit silently through what she had to say, listen to Purdy's probing, then corner her with a single, well-informed comment. So she must be flashy for Purdy, devastatingly accurate for Roy.

She smiled. 'We'll press on, shall we?'

For Purdy's benefit she dropped the names of her most prestigious clients. For Roy's she gave a hard-nosed, step-by-step account of the campaign she proposed – market research, target audience, lead-in times, media mix, follow-up.

At the end of it, at five o'clock, they all shook hands. 'I must say,' said Roy. 'I am most impressed. None of the competitors have the same level of professional expertise.' Purdy added, 'Touch of showmanship about your presentation, too. I like to see that.' Roy concluded, 'Need to have it ratified by the Board. But you can take it as read that you have the contract.'

Gillian returned to her office on a high. This evening, she decided, she would tell the man she met a thing or two.

At seven p.m. she entered the wine bar where she had arranged to rendezvous. She recognised Peter because he was carrying a rolled-up copy of the *Standard* and because his eyes lit with appreciation as she walked in. She tossed the end of her red scarf over her shoulder, flung back her head and strode over to him. He jumped to his feet.

'Gillian, you must be Gillian. I wasn't expecting anyone at all like you.'

'What do you mean? Is there something wrong? I told you what I'd be wearing.'

'Of course not.' He frowned doubtfully. 'You look marvellous. Spot on. Can I get you a drink?'

Gillian sat down. 'Dry white wine,' she said. 'Frascati if they have it.'

Peter returned with a bottle and two glasses. 'White Lambrusco,' he told her. 'It's slightly sparkling so I thought you'd prefer it.' He poured the wine and lit a cigarette for himself. 'I won't offer you one. I'm sure you don't smoke. You look so fit.'

'I am fit. I swim thirty lengths twice a week. I work out with weights for two hours on Saturdays. I walk up all the escalators I come across. Plus I have an extremely high-powered job; I have just signed a contract with a major new client. And I'm Sagittarius but I've never played tennis in my life.'

'I can imagine you in a tennis dress. You have such long legs.'

'My knees are knobbly,' she said firmly. 'Have been since I was a kid.'

Peter said, 'We could have a meal later. I'm sure you like Chinese food.'

'Shall I tell you how much the contract is worth?' asked Gillian. 'Or are you going to tell me what you think of my hair? This isn't my natural colour by the way.'

'It's a lovely colour.'

'Thirty thousand in round figures. See my hands?' She offered him one. 'I used to bite my nails.'

'You can't do now. They're perfect.'

'Plus a generous amount for expenses. Be honest. You prefer shorter women.'

'You said on the phone you didn't mind me being four foot eight.'

'Of course, it's taken me years to get where I am. I did tell you how old I am, didn't I?'

'Yes. You don't look it.'

'What about my nose?' Gillian persisted. 'It's too big, isn't it? I should have had it altered. But I can't afford it. Not even on my salary.'

He looked at her warily. 'It isn't too big. What's wrong? Why do you keep asking me about yourself?'

'Nothing. Nothing's wrong. Could I have one of your cigarettes?'

Unlike the other men, Peter did not suggest they meet again.

But Gillian did not let this faze her. She woke next morning – Saturday – with renewed determination. She combed her hair, applied her make-up and set off for the Post Office. She bought six first-class stamps, took a pound coin from her purse and went into the automatic photo booth. She posed carefully for each exposure. The snaps these machines took never portrayed her at her best, but they would give the general impression. After waiting a few minutes she collected the pictures from the slot outside the booth, put them in her bag without looking at them and hurried home.

In her living room she took the bundle of replies to her ad in the *New Statesman*, settled at her desk and wrote to Michael who was an architect and described himself as outgoing. In her letter she told him about her job, her salary and the contract she had won yesterday. She signed the letter and took the snaps from her bag

She stared at them. Had she picked up someone else's by mistake?

Huge pools of eyes stared back at her from the dead white planes of the face. The nose was large and lumpen; the hair was stringy and unkempt. Dark shadows disfigured the character's chin. It was a photo of a corpse – but it was Gillian's corpse, she had to admit. She looked at the second photo: the person in this one seemed to be dead too. But a shifty, rather criminal smirk, lingered in her eyes.

She dropped the photos, rushed into the bathroom and looked in the mirror. She looked the same as before. She rushed back to the living room and picked up the snaps.

The phone was ringing. It was a man, a new one called Oliver. He began to tell her about himself. 'I'm just over six foot, dark-haired, with a beard, medium build,' he said. 'What do you look like?'

Gillian snorted. 'I've got a dead white face, staring black eyes, stringy hair and I need a shave,' she announced in a rush, put the phone down and collapsed into gales of laughter.

After a while, when the gales dwindled to chortles, Gillian wrote three more letters. In them, she again described the work she did and the success she had achieved; she gave details of her height, weight and false hair colour; she even made a comment or two – as some of the men had in their letters – on her sexual preferences. From time to time she stopped to laugh. Finally, still shaking, she cut the photos apart and clipped one to each letter. These men would know how she really looked.

FRIDAY NIGHT, WATCHING TV

'Hello, who's that?' said Alan's voice at the other end of the line.

'It's Geraldine,' Geraldine said into the phone. 'Thought I'd ring. Just to see how you're doing.'

'Oh, hello. I'm okay actually. How are you?'

'Fine. You're all right then?'

'Sure. How did you know I was here?'

'There was a number on the early news.'

'Did they have a lot about the thing this afternoon?'

'A bit. So you're okay?'

'Will be. Broken my arm. A few cuts. What are you doing this evening?'

'Not a lot. Watching television as usual. You know how I am on Fridays. Have you had people to see you?'

'No need. I'll be out in a day or so. I would have rung if this hadn't happened. Come over to your place perhaps.'

'I could have a couple of hours free tomorrow. If you tell me what to bring.'

'You don't really want people to see you.'

'Oh,' Geraldine paused. 'Right.'

'I could give you a call next Friday. Meet up as usual? Though I think my arm will be in plaster. If that's okay?'

'Of course. That's fine. See you then.'

Geraldine hung up and went into her living room. She looked at her watch. Nearly seven o'clock. The news would be starting on Channel Four. She switched on the television. Alan was on the screen; there were streaks of blood on his face, his arm was strapped up and he wore a blanket round his shoulders. He said, 'One hell of a crash, that's all. Then people rolling around all over the place. No, I couldn't see what caused it. Yes, my left arm was trapped. No, I don't know how long. The Fire Brigade were superb. And I was luckier than some.' Geraldine had seen this shot earlier.

She watched the next scene; nurses running towards a hospital, their unbuttoned navy-blue coats flapping over pale uniforms. A reporter explained, 'NHS staff throughout the south of the city have been recalled to deal with the emergency.' The camera returned to the scene of the disaster, lingered over piles of debris strewn on the railway embankment and focused on firemen cutting through the tangled remains of the trains. Then it showed two of the coaches of the second train sprawled across the track. 'The death toll currently stands at twenty-one, with fifty-four survivors receiving hospital treatment,' said the reporter.

Geraldine hoovered the living room and watered her plants. She picked off the dead leaves one by one. She went into the kitchen, scrambled three eggs and returned to the living room to eat them. It was still only a quarter to eight – exactly the time when, last Friday, Alan turned up. 'Hi,' he said when she opened the front door. 'Good week?' he asked as he followed her into the living room. 'So, so.' Geraldine switched on the television. 'You?' 'About the same.' They sat on the sofa and watched *The Two Ronnies*, laughing at the same jokes.

This Friday Geraldine returned to the kitchen, washed her plate, wiped all the worktops, mopped the floor and cleaned out two cupboards. She unplugged the fridge and opened the door intending to let the fridge defrost. There were two cans of beer inside; she took one.

On the nine o'clock news she watched Alan sitting in bed, wearing striped pyjamas. Geraldine had not seen him in pyjamas before. The next sequence – from an amateur video taken soon after the crash – showed him being cut out of a wrecked coach. He was wearing a leather jacket with one sleeve torn off. Then Geraldine learned:

> lumps of concrete had been found on the line in front of the first train
> Alan had been in the third coach of the second train and was therefore luckier than the people in the first and second coaches, several of whom were dead
> British Rail had introduced new safety measures over the last few months, but they could not legislate against criminal vandalism
> most injuries were to the head or the chest, so Alan's were unusual.

Last week Alan was not in bed at nine o'clock; he was watching the news with Geraldine. When the news finished they bent over the *Guardian* TV page, deciding what to see next. 'It's all rather heavy,' Alan complained. 'Who on earth wants to watch a documentary about heroin addicts in Hong Kong on a Friday night? Or another of those dramas about the Second World War?'

'The *Golden Girls* is on later.'

Geraldine did not watch the *Golden Girls* tonight because it clashed with *News at Ten*. On *News at Ten* Alan was cut from the wrecked coach, then he wore a blanket and said, 'One hell of a crash, that's all,' and then he sat in bed in pyjamas. After that Geraldine learned:

> inspectors from the Department of Transport were at the scene

two survivors had died in hospital
the London Fire Brigade was continuing to work on
the wreckage but did not expect to find anyone else
alive.

Last Friday Geraldine and Alan went to bed after the
Golden Girls. Geraldine was still thinking about who
would want to watch dramas about the Second World
War on a Friday night. 'What would you do if there was
a war?' she asked Alan as they undressed. 'And you had
to fight?'

'Hide.'

She laughed. 'That's cheating. They'd find you.'

'Not if I hid well enough.' He paused and stepped out
of his trousers. 'Or I could pretend to be someone else.'

'Should I pretend that too?'

'If it turns you on.'

Geraldine sat on the bed and thought for a moment.
'I don't think it does,' she said slowly. 'But maybe that's
because you haven't told me who you're planning to be.'

'Mickey Rourke? Charles Dance?'

Mickey Rourke was a possibility because his eyes were
similar to Alan's. Whereas Charles Dance did not re-
semble him in any way. 'I'll think it over,' she said. 'I'll
let you know,' and got into bed.

This Friday Geraldine settled down to wait for *Newsnight*. She decided to sleep on the sofa so as not to miss
anything. No one had mentioned how fast the trains
were going: nor the precise time of impact, not down
to the minute. She wanted to hear interviews with other
survivors and to know what the emergency services had
to say – the fire fighters who rushed to the scene, the
doctors who performed the operations. She wanted to see
reconstructions of the accident, diagrams of how it might
have come about.

After *Newsnight* there was snooker and a film on BBC2. She switched to London Weekend because it went on all night and watched another film, then a comedy about a Los Angeles police precinct. The set was so tacky she expected it to collapse each time one of the characters came through the door. She fell asleep. When she woke her neck was stiff. American football was on the screen.

Ads. The five a.m. news. There was only one development. 'Already last night,' said a reporter, 'commuters were laying flowers beside the track where the crash took place.' People always did that, Geraldine reflected. Strange. Why not give the flowers to the survivors? She imagined herself turning up at Alan's bedside with an armful of freesias and went hot all over. Too hot to go back to sleep.

She picked a bunch of flowers for Alan once. On his birthday. From her garden. Daffodils. It was late March. The air was raw and threatened rain but was tinged with the warmth of spring. The sky was a murky, pinkish grey; clouds swirled across it exposing higher, greyer banks of cloud. She snipped crisp green stalks with a pair of scissors. Milky liquid oozed from the stalks. She had so many daffs in her garden; she could pick loads.

On the bus to Alan's flat she held the flowers carefully in her lap, then lifted them to sniff their faint fragrance. 'What an enormous bunch,' said the woman next to her. 'For your Mum are they?' 'What? Oh yes. Of course,' Geraldine replied and left the bus a stop early.

The woman was right. The bunch was too big. Geraldine checked no one was looking, took one daffodil and dropped it over a wall into a garden. Did the same again. And again. Until the bunch was not too big.

It was too small; it was pathetic. Better to turn up with a single flower. She threw all of them away except one, then realised how silly and significant it would be to arrive on his doorstep with one daffodil; she tucked it into the contents of an overflowing litter bin and arrived at Alan's empty-handed.

They had a good evening together, all the same. She remembered the evening because his parents had given him an awful sweater for his birthday and between comedy programmes on the television she and Alan thought up alternative uses for an awful sweater. The best one was as a skirt, modelled by Geraldine, with the sleeves twisted into a waistband.

At six, TV am started and there was a news round-up every fifteen minutes. Geraldine hardly had time to boil the kettle, to make a cup of coffee, to toast a slice of bread between shots of Alan being rescued, wearing a blanket and sitting up in bed in pyjamas. She was used to seeing him in pyjamas by now; also, by now, she quite understood why he wouldn't really want people to see him. She wouldn't either, if she were him.

THE BALANCE OF TRADE

'In favour of the motion to increase the subsidy on Uridian marioc by sixteen per cent, 522 votes,' announced Neputa Tharm, Leader of the Council of the Galaxy. 'Against the motion, one vote.' The World stood alone.

'How do I feel?' The President of the World turned quickly to Susan. 'Am I shocked by this decision? Am I taken aback?'

'No,' she replied. 'First you are outraged. Thump your fist on the table. Then you are saddened on behalf of the citizens, not just of the World, but of the Galaxy. Shake your head slowly at that point. The sequence of feelings is: anger, dismay, regret, then strong determination.'

The President spoke and spoke well, then sat down.

It was rare for the Leader of the Council to make a proposal; he did so now. 'The Council must of course proceed on the basis of the vote,' he said. 'But the President of the World can have left none of us unmoved by the depth of his feeling. It is within the power of the Council to make a one-off grant to the World for golden hellos to attract a higher calibre of research workers. I believe we would be wrong to do less.'

The Council moved to the vote once more. The proposal was agreed. Neputa Tharm brought the proceedings to an end. The Heads of State rose to their feet.

'A good piece of work, Susan,' said the President of the World.

'Yes, President. It was your delivery. Particularly your timing, switching from regret to determination.'

'Even while I was speaking I realised I could well turn the tables with that. The dinner will be child's play by comparison.'

As always after a plenary session of the Council, the dinner was a formal affair. The medals and chains of office of the Heads of State glittered in the white light from cubic fittings suspended over the tables in the banqueting hall. Waiters in the silver national costume of Luctia bowed stiffly as they placed dish after lavish dish in front of the delegates. Susan wore a high-shouldered gold tube of a dress with a tall collar which restricted the movement of her neck. She sat beside the President.

The Emperor of Trame leant forward from the opposite side of the table. 'A pleasant surprise for you, I imagine, President,' he said. 'You cannot have expected such a satisfactory development for the World at such a late stage in the debate.'

'You are not at all satisfied,' Susan said softly into the President's ear. 'Nor are you pleased. You are surprised that the Council could not do more for the World. But you are cautiously optimistic because of the constructive atmosphere in which the talks took place. You are hopeful of better results at future meetings.'

After the dinner, each of the Heads of State was to be presented with a small Luctian art form. Susan had read of the ceremony in the factual brief for the President (Michael's brief, but she did not allow herself to think of Michael). She had read, 'Art forms are made by the people of Luctia from the preserved arms and legs of the people of Vascar. They are exported in large quantities to Coria.'

The President accepted his scrap of twisted limb with a gracious smile and said, on Susan's advice, 'I am delighted to receive this gift which I see as a symbol of the cultural and commercial interdependence of the planets. I am confident that we shall move forward from this Council to greater co-operation between the planets and thus to mutual gain.'

A nurse switched on the television in the lounge. A voice announced, 'The News, read by Derek Carlisle.' Some of the people sitting at the big table did not even raise their eyes. A woman with long white hair wearing a loose, black dress went on plaiting bright strands of silk; a young, dark man in a sleeveless jerkin continued to bend over the sketch book in which he was drawing. On the screen Derek Carlisle said, 'Our foreign affairs correspondent, Trevor Newsom, is now in the studio on Luctia, ready to explain to us the background to today's decisions by the Council of the Galaxy.' Trevor Newsom's face appeared to one side of Derek's. A small boy in pyjamas put down the basket he was weaving and looked at the face for a second or two, then turned back to his basket.

'Now, Trevor,' Derek Carlisle confronted his colleague, 'we know that the President of the World faced a demand for higher salaries from our research workers; that unless he came up with some incentive we would lose the best of those workers; and that the increased contribution towards marioc manufacture would compete directly for Exchequer funds. But why the need for the increase in the marioc subsidy in the first place?'

A small, fair woman came into the lounge, picked up an embroidery frame from the table, turned a chair away from the television, sat on the chair and began to sew.

'Put simply, Derek,' Trevor replied, 'the production costs of marioc have risen in excess of the price the Martians can afford. The Uridian economy depends on income from marioc sales and the Martian economy would collapse without regular supplies of the drug.'

'But there are other markets for marioc. The World, for instance?'

'Tiny by comparison. In the World, marioc is a luxury enjoyed by the few. But the Martian Government has signed a contract guaranteeing weekly delivery to the Furus – the native tribes of Mars – in return for which the Furus work the red iron mines. This is to the benefit of both parties. The Furus are addicted to marioc and cannot survive without a regular supply. But conditions in the mines are so appalling that if the Furus were not under the influence of the drug they would undoubtedly refuse outright to go below ground.'

'And red iron? How important is that to the balance of trade?'

The dark man stopped drawing. He lifted his picture, held it at arm's length, considered it, replaced it on the table, rubbed out a couple of lines and carried on drawing.

'Essential.' A shot of a factory. Red iron ore poured continuously from a chute into a labyrinthine machine. Several people wearing masks connected by tubes to cylinders strapped to their backs pulled levers and inspected moving parts of the machine. 'Library footage,' said Trevor, 'of a refinery on Trame. Refined red iron is pumped into the breathing apparatus that each inhabitant of Trame wears at all times. With the help of the red iron a Tramen is able to inhale the atmosphere of the planet – which would otherwise be deadly to him – and to exhale gas for export to Vascar. The Vascars have, of course, become headless through repeated exposure to Tramen-exhalation. But the gas also causes them to grow extra arms and legs (at a rate for the average adult male Vascar of one limb every two months, slightly longer for women and children).'

The elderly woman pulled at her silks and a skein fell from her lap. The young, dark man looked at it lying on the floor. He rose, walked round the table and picked up the skein. He touched the woman on her arm and she turned and smiled up at him. He smiled back, dropped the silk in front of her and returned to his drawing.

Trevor went on talking to Derek: 'The Luctians preserve Vascar limbs,' he said. A twisted sculpture appeared on the screen. '. . . and carve them into art forms which the Coriads purchase and contemplate to stimulate their lateral thinking.'

'And the World buys the lateral thinking, of course,' said Derek, 'and we transform it in our research establishments into practical schemes for export to Uridia.'

'Exactly, Derek. Uridia, as a developing planet, is much in need of practical schemes but it could no longer pay for them without today's increase in the subsidy. And without the new grant for golden hellos the World would have lost its research workers. So today's decision on the golden hellos is something of a coup for the President of the World.'

The small fair woman snipped her blue thread with a pair of scissors. She opened a wicker sewing box, looked inside, shook her head and closed the box again. The elderly woman separated a skein of red silk from the bundle in her lap and gave it to her. A second nurse came into the lounge and switched off the news.

It was late, very late. Susan was alone in the double sleeping-space which had been allotted to Michael and her for the night. She took off her shoes. She slipped out of her dress. She went into the adjoining bathroom and soaked in warm, scented water. She smoothed her skin with oil and chose a short, ice-green robe in which to welcome him. She sat down on the bed. It was a long time since she had last seen Michael: it was seven months, two weeks and three days, four if she counted today.

She tried to think about Michael. She was always careful not to think about him during their estrangements but now, with him so near in time, there was a permissible pleasure in doing so. Or perhaps there was a heightened distress? What did she think? That he was tall and broad-shouldered, that his hair was fair and thick, his eyes blue. But what did she feel? To come up with the right emotions for the President of the World, though hard work, was still so much easier than identifying her own. If only she and Michael had more time together, time for her feelings to rise close enough to the surface for her to be sure of what they were.

Michael burst into the sleeping-space. 'Darling,' he boomed, 'you've no idea how much I've missed you.' He kissed her. He removed the green robe. He fucked her. He fell asleep. It didn't matter, thought Susan. Breakfast was bound to arrive early enough for them to have time to talk afterwards.

Sure enough, in the morning, a small round table holding an appetising array of titbits rose from the floor a minute or two before Susan and Michael had finished their exercise routine. It nearly knocked Susan off her balance.

They sat at the table. Michael talked eagerly between mouthfuls. 'So, tell me how you've been, what you've been doing. Before here, I mean. I know all about the marioc debate. I wrote the President's factual brief, did you realise that?'

'I saw your name on the front page.' She wondered whether to say that she had missed him.

'What was it like on the galactic tour of state?' he went

on. 'What did you make of Pollux? Are conditions there as primitive as everyone says?'

'Pretty much,' she said instead. 'How about you? How have you been?'

'Hectic, as ever. I managed to hammer out the brief for the marioc debate in the nick of time. The final information turned up late and we were at it till the small hours. Still, glad to hear that it pulled the President through.'

'Tell you something else,' he said. Susan watched him take a large bite of a Luctian yeast cake. She watched him drain his cup and thump it onto the table. 'You'll never believe who I came across during the talks on Zork.'

How did Michael feel, Susan wondered. How did he feel about being here with her?

Michael leaned towards her. 'Go on. Guess.'

He felt cheerful, she decided. Perhaps he even felt happy.

'I don't know.'

'James. James Cardiff. You remember him. Chap with red hair. Same year as us in college. Quite an old flame of yours.'

'James? He was the first man I ever thought of partnering.' She watched as Michael frowned and leant back. 'Never seriously, of course,' she added quickly. 'Is he stationed on Zork?'

'Far from it. He was taking advantage of one of the training schemes. Said it got him out of the rut for a while. He hasn't worn too well, to be honest. And he's still living in the World. Sorting out the boundary dispute between Russia and the United States.'

'James? In local government? How did he feel about that?'

'No idea. I always said I'd make you a better partner, didn't I? Think where you'd be if you'd chosen him.'

Susan made an effort to imagine what it would be like to live a settled life with a partner she saw every day. She could not imagine it.

'We've come a long way, you and I,' Michael went on. 'What's more, we're still going places.'

Susan said, 'I'm leaving for Trame tomorrow for the bilaterals. Just for two weeks before we have our home leave together.'

'Aha,' said Michael. 'I've some news too. I've been saving it. I'm in for promotion again. Second Comptroller on Gibor. The President told me in person last night. That's why I was so late.' He paused and frowned again. 'Don't I deserve any congratulations?'

'Michael of course you do. It's wonderful. You must be, you must be . . . pleased. You must be delighted: and excited: you must be looking forward to it. When do you start?'

'Right away. It means our not having our leave together. But you don't mind, do you? After all, it's for us.' He looked at his watch. 'I must dash. I want to catch one of the Uridian delegates before he leaves.' He tightened his tie, put on his jacket, picked up his case. 'Onwards and upwards,' he said, bending to kiss her. 'I'll write as usual as soon as I arrive.'

In the lounge of the residential home the white-haired woman was moulding a lump of clay. Around her head she wore, Furu-fashion, the bright band she had woven from the silks. The boy sat on the floor beside her, carving a piece of balsa wood. The dark man was also on the floor, kneeling. He stirred a pot of paint, dipped a brush in the paint, bent forward and applied it in slow strokes to the sheet of card in front of him. The boy turned and pointed to the woman's headband. She unwound it and gave it to him. He smoothed it with his fingers. She took it and tied it round his brow. He lifted the object he was carving, lifted it with both hands to show to her. It was a boat.

As before, the news was on. 'We are now going live to Luctia,' said Derek Carlisle. A vast auditorium appeared on the screen; every seat was filled; at the far end was a platform. '. . . where the formal press conference to mark the end of the Council of the Galaxy is about to begin.'

The picture changed to a close-up shot of the platform. The table on it held a thicket of microphones, a glass and a jug of water. Behind the table sat the President of the World. Beside the President sat Susan.

'You have already been given a full briefing on the facts,' said the President. 'Now is your opportunity to put to me any questions you have on the detailed implications for the people of the World of the Council's decisions.'

'Could you tell us, President,' Trevor Newsom asked the question, 'how you would describe your feelings when the marioc vote went against you?'

The President turned to Susan. There was a pause; the President dipped his head and spoke into the microphones.

'Lonely,' said the President.

He frowned and turned back to Susan. She nodded and he went on, 'I was lonely. I was not satisfied. I was not pleased. I was surprised that the Council could not do more for the World. But I am cautiously optimistic about the atmosphere in which the talks were conducted. I am hopeful for better results at future councils. I am lonely yes, but my loneliness is the price I pay in order that the people of the World may look ahead to peace and freedom and to a decent standard of living for their children.'

Susan said, loudly enough for her words to be clearly audible, 'That is not what I said President. I said that I am lonely.'

Two nurses wheeled a trolley into the lounge, blocking the television screen from the view of the people in the room. 'Time for tea everybody,' said one of the nurses brightly.

'I still don't understand how you could do such a thing,' Michael complained. 'With your emotional experience. Especially as my promotion could go by the board.'

Susan did not answer. She looked away from him, out of the car window, seeing nothing. Tears filled her eyes; they rolled down her cheeks and dropped from her chin. She cried silently, but made no effort to stop, although Michael would not like to see her cry.

'I shouldn't have said that,' he went on. 'I'm sorry, darling. It's not your fault. A few weeks back here in the World won't do my career serious harm. It's your health that matters. I'll find another post as soon as you're better.'

He drove on. 'Can you tell me where to take a left?' he asked after a while. 'It should be somewhere near here.' He turned his head towards her. 'You're crying. Why are you crying?' But Susan could not say.

'It's a good thing we've booked you into this place,' Michael continued. 'You know you need professional help. And it's supposed to be the best in the World. We've the President to thank for that. He thinks very highly of you, you know. He wouldn't pick up the tab for anyone else. It's not just the medical attention that's first class either; there's a gym, so you won't give up your exercise routine will you, darling? And a swimming pool. Ah, this must be it.'

There were several people in the room, Susan saw. Maybe as many as ten. One of them was making a basket;

another was drawing; they were all doing something. None of them looked up when she and Michael entered. There was a television in one corner of the room. Its screen was blank. Susan sat on a chair close to the screen. She saw some shadows on its surface, smears of cleaning fluid perhaps. The smears made the shape of a winged lizard, only it had no proper nose. Susan tilted her head. Looked at from this new angle, the smears were only smears. She counted them; she lost count. There were either five smears or six. She counted them again, then realised that Michael was saying goodbye.

'Hate to leave you with this bunch of weirdos. That old woman looks like a witch. Something decidedly peculiar about the boy with the whatsit round his head. And there's a grown man sitting on the floor over there. Look on the bright side, though. At least you have a private room. And you'll soon be out of here in any case. Back at the President's side where you belong. I'll be in to see you tomorrow, darling.'

'It's a lovely morning.' The nurse pulled back the curtains. 'We'll have everyone out and about today. You could take a stroll in the grounds. Or have a swim. It's up to you.'

Susan walked in a small, formal garden. She paced the garden; she found it was an exact square. She stopped and looked at the garden; inside the square was a circle of flower beds. Low clipped hedges enclosed the beds. The circle was divided into four equal segments by two straight paths; she took one of the paths. At the intersection of the paths she came to a fountain. Near the fountain several people sat on canvas chairs, sewing. One of them nodded a greeting to Susan. Susan nodded back. At the end of the garden she reached a summerhouse. Inside the summerhouse she saw an old woman and a boy. The boy held out something to Susan. It was a boat, a wooden boat for miniature Vikings, with a curved prow and a square sail of bright, woven silk. The old woman was making a clay animal; the animal was a little like a lion, but it was not a lion. It was a gryphon, Susan decided. She walked on. Behind the summerhouse, on a stretch of grass, sat a man, cross-legged. His back was towards her. She walked round him. He was painting a picture. She walked round him again. He did not look up. She returned to the formal garden and paced its perimeter several times, counting her steps to see if the number would be the same on each circuit; but it wasn't. She went indoors to her room, lay on the bed and looked at the ceiling until a nurse brought lunch.

In the afternoon Susan sat alone in the lounge. The smears on the television had gone so she gazed at the reflection of the sunlight on the blank screen instead. The door of the room opened. A nurse said, 'Time for you to see the doctor.' Susan followed her along the corridor. A plump man in a three-piece suit shook Susan's hand. 'How are you feeling?' he asked, but she did not answer.

'How are you feeling?' asked Michael afterwards. He was waiting for her in the lounge. On the television in front of them the President of the World said abruptly, 'It's not a question of how I feel. The fact is that we have no option but to raise salaries. The one-off grant was not enough to retain our researchers. We will therefore be unable to pay our contribution to the marioc subsidy. The Council of the Galaxy must make some concession. It's as simple as that.'

A close-up of Neputa Tharm followed. 'The President of the World,' he said, 'spoke with great feeling at the last meeting of the Council. But it is clear from the tone of his recent statements that the issue no longer concerns him deeply. We will give no further grant.'

'The President's not the same without you,' said Michael. 'He's losing his touch.'

Susan's days fell into a pattern. In the mornings she walked in the formal garden. When the group of people were sewing by the fountain they nodded to her and she nodded back. When the old woman and the boy were in the summerhouse they looked up and smiled and showed her what they were making. Then Susan walked past the summerhouse to watch the dark man paint. She stood for hours behind him, seeing him sketch, then stop and change what he had drawn. She walked round him, but he never raised his head. In the afternoons she sat in the lounge, sometimes on her own, sometimes with the others; but if the others were there she did not look at them, only at the television screen. Nor did she nod to them or smile or turn to see whether the dark man was there and whether he was painting. Michael might come to visit her at any time.

'Don't try to talk,' he said when he came. 'You're not up to it. I'll tell you what's happening outside. The marioc shortage – that's the main thing these days. The authorities have set a limit of one twist per customer per week, which is no way to handle the problem. They'll end up with panic buying and stockpiling and blackmarket trading. You know we only imported a small amount but all the same there was always enough to meet demand. Makes me glad I never touched the stuff.' He had always put two pinches of it on his food, hadn't he? thought Susan but she wasn't sure and Michael was talking again. 'I blame the emotional advisers. I gather one of them told the President he should be downcast during his negotiations with Uridia. Even I can see that he should have been implacable.'

On the screen there were scenes of rioting and looting. Wild-eyed Furus, bright scarves knotted round their brows, hurled chunks of red iron ore through the plate-glass windows of Government House. 'Bit of crisis on Mars, isn't there?' asked Michael. 'Now the Uridians can't afford to produce enough marioc for the government there to keep the Furus sweet.'

Next day, behind the summerhouse, the dark man began to colour in his picture – he used two colours only, yellow and blue. The picture was of a terraced garden. There were steps from one terrace to another but Susan could not yet see where they would lead in the end. Perhaps to the distant yellow castle? In the foreground, blue water tumbled beside the steps into rectangular pools.

Still the man did not look up. Susan wondered how she would feel if he did; or if she touched him or let him know in some other way that she was there?

'It's really time you snapped out of it, whatever it is,' said Michael in the lounge later. 'I've even had a letter from the President's office asking for your date of return. And look what's going on.' He waved his hand towards the TV.

'Martial law has been declared on Mars,' announced Derek Carlisle. 'All mining of red iron has ceased. We are going over to Trame to see what effect this is having.' Tramens lay in the streets, in offices, in their homes, gasping, choking, clutching their throats, fighting for air. 'As yet there have been no fatalities,' said Trevor Newsom, stepping in front of a group of writhing Tramens. 'But without the resumption of a regular supply of red iron, it can only be a matter of time before these tragic people die.'

How did Susan feel about that? she wondered.

'It's all such a mess,' said Michael. 'If you could only get over it. Though I'm worried about you first and foremost, of course.' She looked at him. His eyes were bright, his smile false. Perhaps he had found a new temporary partner by now.

'If relations between the planets don't improve the Council may break up altogether,' he went on. 'I could be out of a job. So could you.'

Next day, on the stretch of grass behind the summer-house, Susan touched the dark man's shoulder. The fabric of his jerkin was rough and stiff. He turned towards her. He raised his eyes and smiled. He stretched out his right hand. Susan saw a smear of yellow paint across his knuckles. She watched his hand approach her face, felt it touch her cheek. His hand was warm; he pulled her face to his face with his warm hand. His lips touched Susan's. They were warm too. The sun was bright; Susan closed her eyes and was in darkness. She opened them and was in the light. She lay on the grass, beside him, and looked up at the blue sky. She watched him move between her and the sky. She lay in the sun on the grass with the dark man.

'I can't stay in the World indefinitely,' said Michael the next day. 'I have my future to think about.' He said this so loudly Susan jumped.

'You did hear me then. Why don't you say anything? You haven't spoken a word to me since you came here.' He looked at his watch. 'The news will be on. Will these people notice if I turn up the sound?'

'Details are just reaching us of a major breakthrough in the Martian revolution,' Derek Carlisle announced. 'In return for a cessation of violence, amnesties have been granted to the Furus and a number of them are to be co-opted onto the Government. The Furus have agreed to return to work – for wages instead of marioc – on condition that it is not in the red iron mines. The red iron mines are therefore to close. The Furus, after the recent prolonged disruption of their marioc supply, have lost their craving for the drug. The total collapse of the Martian market for marioc is expected to have a major effect on the economy of Uridia.'

Loud music flooded the room; on the screen people were dancing, as far as the eye could see. 'I am standing in what until very recently was one of the largest Uridian marioc manufacturing centres,' Trevor Newson poked his microphone in front of the nearest dancer. 'How do you feel about the loss of Uridia's main market for marioc?' he shouted above the music. 'Terrific. All the more for us. Join the party,' the dancer replied.

The picture changed once more. 'Yes, a remarkable discovery,' said the Emperor of Trame. 'If we breathe through our pores instead of the apparatus we have no problem at all. And we all feel so much better.'

In the morning Susan watched as the dark man made the steps in the picture higher and steeper. The steps were in flights, with platforms at intervals which would allow her to stop and rest. She would be panting, longing to reach the top. What would she see when she arrived? She touched his shoulder as she had the day before. He looked up at her and smiled and she lay down with him on the grass in the sun.

Michael did not visit the next day, nor the day after. On the third day Susan received a letter from him in which he explained that he was in a clinic for marioc addicts, 'Not that I could be called an addict,' he wrote, 'and this place is more of a health farm, really.'

That afternoon Susan sat in the lounge with the other people. She looked at them one by one; she nodded to the people she had seen sewing by the fountain; she smiled at the old woman and the boy. She rose, crossed the room and sat with the dark man on the floor.

On the TV screen was a crowded room; smartly-dressed people sipped cocktails; they talked with animation. 'As a Vascar,' said Trevor Newsom to a woman in a purple, off-the-shoulder frock, 'you must surely regret that you can no longer grow the extra arms and legs on which your livelihood depends?'

'Not a bit of it,' The woman laughed. 'As you can see, now that we have stopped exposing ourselves to Tramen-exhalation we have developed heads and can talk to each other for the first time. We're all discovering conversation. No market for it of course, but what the Hell? Now, who can I introduce you to?'

'There are changes on Luctia, too.' The television showed two children chasing each other round a car, shrieking. A woman and a man were packing a hamper, blankets and Wellingtons into the car. 'Trevor Newsom,' said Derek Carlisle, 'is now on Luctia, having just arrived from Vasca where he earlier recorded the interview we have just seen.'

An exhausted-looking Trevor walked into the picture. He approached the man. 'Today is Tuesday,' he said, 'a working day. Could you tell us why you are not at work?'

The man replied. 'Nothing to preserve now the Vascars have no limbs to sell to us. May as well live in the present, that's what I say. You ought to have a day off yourself.'

'Where are you going?'

'To the mountains.'

'No,' cried the children. 'Let's go to the sea.'

'Oh, let's,' said the woman.

The man said. 'Quickly, then. Run and fetch your swimsuits. Before the sun goes in.'

After that two giggling Coriads appeared. They had their arms around each other. 'Fuck lateral thinking,' said one of them. 'We're going to have a shot at making love sideways instead.'

Finally, a press conference. 'A question for the President of the World.' (Trevor Newsom is speaking to the President by satellite from Luctia, interposed Derek Carlisle.) 'How do you feel about the collapse of inter-planetary trade?' asked Trevor. 'Are you weary of the endless round of new developments? Are you exhausted by the continuing, surprising sequence of events? Are you burned out? Are you finished?' And the President replied, 'No. I am disappointed. I am resolute. No. I am implacable. I am outraged. Angry. Optimistic. Yes, I am optimistic. And confident. And taken aback.' A nurse came into the room and switched off the news.

Susan looked at the dark man's picture. The yellow steps rose in steep flights but now it was clear that when she reached the top she would also be at the bottom, starting out. The blue water which tumbled down formal cascades fell through several levels but the lowest level fed into the highest. Susan did not know how she felt about this until she saw that he had painted himself and herself half-way up or half-way down, looking up or down at their reflections in the water. She felt that she would like to take up life drawing. Either that or sculpture.

AVOIDING GATWICK

Saturday morning and Sara was packing. Books first –
the new Fay Weldon, an Alan Coren paperback collection
and a weighty Zoë Oldenburg. Then a pack of cards, and
backgammon, Trivial Pursuit and Monopoly because she
was sure the cottage would have only Snakes and Ladders
and jigsaws with several pieces missing. For the daytimes
she would need swimsuit, snorkel and flippers; oilskin,
so rain could not stop her going out; Hunter boots and
crash cap because she was bound to find a riding stable;
tennis racquet – on the offchance, as Rodney didn't play;
a frisbee; a lilo; shorts, walking boots, a pedometer, a
compass, a small knapsack and a thermos. Oh, and she
would take the folding bike.

She went downstairs to the kitchen where Rodney
was packing food and cookery equipment into cartons.
'Surely you won't need the fish kettle?' she queried. She
opened the cutlery drawer. 'What have you done with the
spanners? I put one in here yesterday.'

'It's not where they belong. Why do you want a
spanner?'

'For the bike. If I fold it up it'll fit in the back of the car.'

'You can't. We won't be able to take the second case of
wine.'

Sara sighed. She said, '(a) it hardly takes up any room once it's folded. (b) if you take the aubergines, artichokes and courgettes out of those boxes and put them in the glove compartment, on the back shelf, wedge them between other things on the floor, there will be loads of space. Presumably the tool kit does still live in the cupboard under the stairs?' He nodded.

At least they wouldn't be bored this year, Sara reflected as she rummaged in the kit. Holidays could be difficult. She sometimes thought that if they went somewhere hot and beachy as most people did – the Seychelles, the Maldives, the Caribbean – they would spend the whole day swimming or sunbathing. But they had long since agreed that there was nowhere to touch the English countryside. Plus none of that awful hassle at Gatwick. She found a spanner and set to work on the bike. But this year, she thought with satisfaction, she was well-prepared; and Rodney had found a much larger place than usual and invited all and sundry to join them.

She returned to the kitchen and replaced the spanner in the cutlery drawer. 'On second thoughts,' she said, taking it out again. 'I'll need it for the bike when we arrive. Incidentally, I'm ready. We did agree we'd start before twelve.'

Late afternoon. Rodney was not in the best of tempers because (he kept saying) he couldn't see out of the rear window with that damned bicycle in the way. Sara was not in the best of tempers because (she kept saying) she had nowhere to put her feet between the aubergines and the case of wine on the floor. But they were nearly there. They turned off the main road and caught sight of the cottage. It was a glorious cottage. Its walls were of pinkwashed cob, its roof was thatched and it stood on its own. Behind were purple moors; in front were the cliffs and the sea.

Rodney pulled up outside the cottage. Sara jumped out of the car, ran through the garden and opened the front door. 'Exposed beams,' she called excitedly over her shoulder. 'A huge fireplace. And chintz curtains.' She opened another door and found a proper farmhouse kitchen, large and homely, with quarry tiled floor, scrubbed table and four chairs. Rodney joined her. As usual he made small disappointing discoveries in the kitchen drawers. 'Only three saucepans and the frying pan is too thin for stir-fry. No salad bowl. Good job I remembered the garlic press. But roughing it a bit is part of the fun.' 'I'm going to look upstairs,' said Sara, 'and choose our room.' 'Make it the one with the hardest bed,' he responded. 'Otherwise it's up to you.'

Sara inspected each of the three bedrooms. The first was scarcely large enough to qualify as a room. Its ceiling sloped and it held a narrow bed with a small table beside it; no space for anything else. The second had a double bed but was at the back of the cottage and overlooked an overgrown vegetable patch. The third was big and light, contained a cupboard, a chest of drawers and twin beds which Sara did not try. She looked out of the window; the view was of the sea. 'We're sleeping in the front. Are you ready to explore?' she called to Rodney, joyously, as she ran down the narrow stairs. But Rodney replied that he wanted to work out which utensils he could improvise with and make a start on the boeuf bourguignon.

Sara stood in the road and inhaled warm, clean country air in which she could distinguish the smell of the sea from a hint of the gorse on the hills. She set off, passing a field of cows on her left, until she reached a gate to a grassy track. Walks across the moors she thought, beginning to plan her activities for the week.

For now she stuck to the road which took her to the right, towards the sea. She walked almost to the edge of the cliff, where the road made a sharp left. Ahead lay a steep, narrow valley and a village, diminutive at this distance, its buildings clustered round a harbour. Below, uneven steps carved out of the cliff led down to a small sandy cove. Sara was pleased with the cove. It was close enough to the cottage for her to take an early morning dip or a quick swim before dinner. At the far end a rocky promontory extended into deep water – a promising place for snorkelling. She turned to walk back, then decided to jog.

A second car was parked outside the cottage. In the kitchen she found Rodney stirring the contents of two saucepans and Veronica, John and a young man she did not know sitting at the table drinking wine. 'Hello all,' Sara said.

'Where did you get to?' Rodney looked up crossly. 'I could have done with a hand.'

'This is Peter,' Veronica announced. 'Lovely to see you, Sara.'

'And you. I was exploring, Rodney. Do I get a drink? Hello, Peter,' but Peter didn't reply.

John poured her a glass of wine. 'Peter's just split up with his partner. Have to bear with him. Great place this. You look as though it's done you good already.'

'There are a few drawbacks.' Rodney began to serve rice. 'No tablespoons, for a start,' brandishing the dessert-spoon he was using. 'And I found a list of rules pinned to the larder door. It says no smoking in the house; if we break anything we have to pay for it; if we make any calls there's a money box beside the phone; no dogs in the lounge, though that won't affect us; the tables in the living room mark easily so use a coaster if you take your drink in there. And we can't light a fire, the chimney hasn't been swept.' He dipped a spoon into the boeuf bourguignon. 'Sara, how about being useful? Making the salad?'

'I'll do it.' Veronica rose from her chair. She washed a Cos lettuce, leaf by leaf, then patted each of them carefully with a tea towel.

'That's the way,' Rodney approved. 'Sara always forgets

to dry them separately.'

'But it's essential! Otherwise the dressing won't adhere.'

After dinner they agreed that Rodney should not wash up. Peter produced a bottle of Bacardi, poured himself a large measure, added some coca cola, looked in the fridge, commented gloomily, 'No ice,' and followed Rodney into the living room. John issued instructions. 'I'll wash, Sara, you dry.' Veronica added that she'd put away later and went to join the others.

John and Sara sang Buddy Holly songs while they worked: 'Words of Love' and 'Peggy Sue' and 'Peggy Sue Got Married.' By the time they started 'I Guess it Doesn't Matter Anymore' they were onto the last saucepan and the table was covered with clean, dry things. 'Do you remember, baby, last September how you held me ti-ight each and every ni-ight?', they sang as the back door opened and Nick came in, a bottle of wine in each hand. 'We-ell whoops a daisy, how you drove me crazy,' sang Nick, pirouetting and waving the bottles in the air, 'but I guess it doesn't matter anymore.' And he dumped the wine on the table with a crash. A clean glass fell onto its side, rolled off the table onto the quarry tiles and shattered.

'What on earth's going on?' Rodney appeared in the living room doorway. 'Oh hello, Nick. Glad you made it. We'll have to pay for that. Where's Carla?' She followed Nick into the room and held out a bunch of sweet peas, wrapped in paper. 'We brought you these, Sara. Stopped specially at a stall by the side of the road. Aren't they lovely?' A few overblown petals drifted to the floor. 'My fault,' said Nick as a big, yellow dog bounced through the door. 'You've met The Hound before, haven't you?' 'Mind his paws on the glass,' Carla warned. Nick pushed the dog into the living room and shut the door behind it. He gestured at the bottles. 'Shall I open these? To restore the peace.' He began to do so. 'If not the pieces.' Then everyone went into the living room, leaving Sara to sweep up.

When she joined them Rodney was making another announcement. 'There's one double room to spare, one single and the floor in here. Sara and I are in the front bedroom. Apart from that I leave you to make your own sleeping arrangements. Nick, the dog isn't allowed in here.'

'It was only because of the glass. I'll put a mat in the kitchen for him later. Would anyone prefer whisky?'

Next morning Sara woke to find Rodney asleep and early sunshine seeping between the curtains. Downstairs she stepped past two sleeping bodies in the living room and closed the front door quietly behind her. One of the cows mooed as she passed their field. She reached the cliff and scrambled down the steps to the beach. The sea was so cold she had to force herself to take the plunge. She swam, as strongly as she could, twice across the cove. It was the perfect start – the real start – to the week.

She returned to the cottage. The smell of fresh coffee and frying bacon filled the kitchen. Rodney was standing at the cooker. The others were sitting at the table. Veronica lit a cigarette. 'No smoking,' he turned, spatula in hand. 'One of the rules of the house.' 'Nonsense,' Veronica replied, 'we can give the place a good airing before we go.' Sara began to look for a cup. 'In that case I'll have one too,' Nick took a pack of Silk Cut from his pocket. Sara found a dirty mug on the draining board and washed it. 'If you must smoke you could at least go in the living room while I'm cooking,' said Rodney. 'Who asked for two eggs and a sausage?' 'I did,' said John. The smokers left.

Sara poured coffee and sat down. 'Did you sleep well, John?' she asked. 'Not too bad. Bed was a bit hard.' Rodney cracked two eggs into the frying pan. 'I'm not doing this every morning,' he said. 'With so many of us we ought to set a rota for cooking. And for chores. Before we even decide what to do today.' 'Fit me in where you need,' said Sara. 'I'm taking the bike to the village.'

In the event she cycled much further, because she was given directions in the village to a riding stable. By the time she found it, booked a ride for the next day and searched – without success – for tennis courts, and pushed the bike up the steep hill which led to the cottage, it was mid-afternoon. She stopped to catch her breath, heard voices, crossed the strip of grass and looked over the cliff. The others – Rodney and Veronica in the lead – were straggling up the steps from the cove. She waited for them and told Rodney, 'I booked a horse for tomorrow afternoon.' 'Good for you,' he said, and turned to Veronica. 'You must tell me what you think of the terrine. We'll have it as the first course this evening.'

Sara mounted her bicycle and rode back to the cottage. She changed into her swimsuit and returned to the cove for a quick dip. She was back again, wriggling out of her wet swimsuit in the bedroom when Rodney came in. He said, 'You're down to lay the table in a few minutes.' Sara fastened her bra and pulled on her shirt. Rodney sat on the bed. 'And,' he added, 'you're part of the shopping expedition tomorrow morning.'

Sara went to bed immediately after dinner. She set the alarm. After all that exercise she might sleep too long. She didn't, but in the morning as she snapped off the alarm, anxious not to wake Rodney, she saw that the man in the next bed was not Rodney, nor was he asleep.

'It's no big deal.' Peter rolled onto his side and shrugged the covers over his shoulder. 'Besides I'm gay.'

'Where's Rodney?'

'Playing Monopoly last time I saw him. Only he and Veronica left in the game. Must have been two o'clock in the morning. We gave up on them.'

Sara dressed in the bathroom. She took a long time to dress. She wanted to bike along the road for a swim but after she finished dressing she simply sat on the edge of the bath and looked out of the window. It was gone eight before there was a knock on the door. 'Anybody in there?' John's voice called. She opened the door. 'You look fresh as a daisy which is more than can be said for the rest of us.' said John. 'Is everyone up?' she asked. 'Far as I know, yes. Veronica's started breakfast.'

In the kitchen she found Veronica cooking and Rodney sitting at the table writing a list. 'You're in charge of this, Sara. Make sure you don't miss anything.'

'Aren't you coming?'

'Veronica and I are going to look for mushrooms.'

After breakfast John wanted to explore, so Nick drove Sara, Carla and Peter into the nearest town. They parked in a 'Pay and Display'. Nick and Peter went in search of an off-licence. Carla went to find craft shops and Sara went to buy Rodney's provisions on her own.

It wasn't easy. Many of the items were unobtainable. She couldn't find coriander, only English parsley. No Chinese leaves, only Iceberg lettuce.

Back at the cottage she found Rodney and Veronica in the kitchen picking over a pile of fungi. Rodney looked up as Sara and the others trooped in. 'We've got quite a haul. Mainly horse mushrooms, but a handful of parasols too.'

Sara asked, 'Where did you get to last night?'

'One or two of these mushrooms are deliquescing already,' Rodney picked out a couple and put them in a plastic bag. 'We decided to have a rota for the beds as well,' he went on, still inspecting the mushrooms. 'Otherwise the same two people have to sleep on the floor all week. I thought of making soup with these, but we'd lose the delicacy of the flavour.'

'You mean there'll be someone different in the bed next to me tonight?'

''Fraid not. You're down for the floor. It's perfectly comfortable if you use the cushions from the armchairs. I could bake them – what do you think, Veronica? Maybe with twists of bacon. How does that sound for lunch?'

'I don't have time for lunch,' said Sara. 'I'm due for my ride.'

Sara's legs were trembling with exhaustion by the time she reached the stables. A girl in breeches led out a grey horse and said, 'I'm Fay. This is Pepper. If you like to get on I'll fetch my horse.'

Fay and Sara rode up a steep track. As they climbed higher the air became cooler and a light breeze rustled the gorse beside the track. Pepper lifted his head, snorted and jogged. They reached the open moors. Fay asked, 'Okay to canter?' and they were off. The horses took clumps of gorse and two stone walls in their stride; they ripped through a copse. Sara ducked her head to dodge low branches; brambles tore at her legs. They came to the edge of the moors and turned down a steep track towards the beach. Stones spurted from the horses' hooves and then they were on a wide stretch of sand, galloping full speed, flying in the face of the wind; the sea, the sky, the cliffs streamed past Sara's stinging cheeks.

'Nice ride?' Rodney asked later as Sara came into the living room of the cottage. 'I've been telling Veronica about the week we had in Scotland. Remember the fresh salmon?'

'Yes thanks. Yes I remember. I'm exhausted.'

'You look wonderful,' said John, 'glowing with health. Shall I pour you a cup of tea? It's just made.'

'Thanks.' Sara dumped herself on the sofa. 'Been swimming?' she asked Carla who was curled in an armchair, wrapped in a purple towel. 'How was the water?'

'I've just had a bath.'

'You could do with one yourself, Sara,' commented

Rodney. 'I can smell horse from the other side of the room. You sitting on the sofa is as bad as letting the dog on it.'

Sara felt better after a cup of tea. She went upstairs, changed into her swimsuit and set off, on foot, for the cove. She plunged into the sea, grateful for the buoyancy of the salt water, then decided to push herself, swam the width of the cove six times and stumbled out onto the sand, shivering.

Back in the cottage she found everyone in the kitchen. Rodney was standing at one end of the table, a turquoise can in his hand.

'Who on earth bought this?' he asked.

Sara said, 'It said beans. On the list.'

He turned to look at her. 'I might have known it was you. It said pinto beans. I was going to make baked beans for tomorrow lunch.'

'Those are baked beans. I often have them when you're not back.'

'Real beans. Home-made baked beans. They take eighteen hours all told, including the overnight soaking. You know that perfectly well. And another thing. Somebody bought honey instead of molasses.'

'They're both natural sweeteners. I was in a hurry.'

'A hurry? This is a holiday, or hadn't you noticed? And have you forgotten you're down to cook tonight?'

'So am I.' It was John who spoke. 'We haven't even started. How about going out for a meal instead?'

'We go out on the last night,' said Rodney.

'We can do that too. Live dangerously. I'll find a place in the phone book and book a table.'

'You won't need the phone book. I brought the *Good Food Guide*. Don't forget to put 10p in the box.'

They went in Nick's car and Rodney and Sara's car. In Rodney and Sara's car were Rodney, Sara, Veronica and John. Rodney drove, Veronica sat in the front. 'What's this on the floor?' she asked. 'It's probably an aubergine,' Sara replied.

At the restaurant they were ushered into a small, extremely hot cocktail lounge. Sara looked at her watch. It was eight thirty-five. 'I thought you booked for eight-thirty, John.' 'I did. They're always behind in this sort of place. What would you like to drink?'

She chose a dry martini because it would have an olive she could eat. She sat in a corner on an antique settle as far away as possible from the blazing open fire. John sat beside her. Rodney opened a large, red menu. 'I'd steer clear of the fruit soup,' he advised Veronica. 'No reason I can see not to try the goulash.' Nick studied the wine list. 'They've a Bulgarian red. That should go with most things.' They all ordered. John talked to Sara but she didn't listen, just nodded from time to time. When at last a waiter said 'Your table is ready,' Sara looked at her watch again and found that it was nine-fifteen.

Ages later, Rodney leant across Veronica. 'Sara, do this with your Access.' Sara did. They would all chip in later, of course, but she was too shattered right now, they must all be too shattered right now, to start doing sums, working out who had eaten what and how much it had cost.

Not too shattered when they arrived at the cottage to propose a round of Trivial Pursuit. Nick poured glasses of whisky. He had forgotten the coasters, Sara noticed. But Rodney had not noticed, he was so deep in conversation with Veronica. Also the dog was sitting on the carpet on Carla's bare feet.

Sara longed to sleep. Unfortunate that it was her turn for the floor. In the end she found a couple of blankets and the alarm clock and curled up regardless. Voices continued for hours, snapping her to occasional attention. 'A googly,' said one. 'The *Daily Mirror*,' said another. 'Ypres,' 'Michaelangelo,' 'Morse Code,' 'Tar-macadam.'

In the night Sara woke to find Rodney's arms round her. 'Not now,' she protested groggily, 'I need my sleep.' But he kissed her just the same. He was not Rodney. She stumbled to her feet, crossed the dark room and switched on the light. John was sitting on the floor in a tangle of blankets. 'You should have said earlier,' he complained. 'You were much more agreeable in the restaurant.' She picked up the alarm clock, three large cushions and a blanket, went into the kitchen and closed the door firmly behind her. She arranged her cushions on the floor with the alarm clock beside them, switched out the light and slipped under the blanket. The Hound snuggled down next to her.

It was just after seven-thirty when Sara woke. The Hound was lying on her arm. She pushed it off, rose and went to look out of the window to see what the weather was like.

It was raining; by the look of the heavy, grey sky it would rain all day. She filled the kettle and switched it on. She opened the door to the living room; John was fast asleep. She climbed the stairs and peered into the room she had chosen for Rodney and herself. Nick was in one bed, Carla in the other. She tiptoed past them to the chest of drawers, took out a pair of shorts and a sweatshirt and slipped back downstairs to the kitchen. She splashed her face with cold water at the sink; she dressed, made a sandwich, filled her thermos with coffee, packed a compass and a map into her knapsack, laced her walking boots and fixed her pedometer to her belt. She took her oilskin from the hook on the back door, buttoned herself into it and stepped out, still undetected.

She strode past the field of cows and turned up the grassy track. Soon she was in the moors. The rain fell steadily; wet bracken brushed her bare legs. She stopped in the shelter of a stone wall, drank a cup of coffee, consulted the map and decided to aim for a twenty-five mile circuit which would bring her out, eventually, at the foot of the steep hill near the village. She rose to her feet and walked on; every so often she checked her pedometer, as she clocked up five, ten, fifteen miles.

It was still raining hours later when Sara returned to the cottage. She was cold and tired; the oilskin had kept her shoulders dry but her socks were drenched and the turn-ups of her shorts flapped wetly against her knees.

She found the kitchen empty. She hung her oilskin on the hook, left her muddy boots on a piece of newspaper and went into the living room. Peter and Nick were sitting on the sofa sharing a bottle of whisky with Sara's backgammon board between them. Carla was cross-legged on the floor next to the coffee table on which she was playing Patience with Sara's cards. Rodney was in an easy chair; Veronica perched on its arm. He was reading aloud from Sara's Alan Coren collection. He stopped reading when he saw her. 'You look as though you got wet.'

'I'm going to have a bath.'

'You can't.' Nick looked up from the backgammon board. 'John is.'

'You're still down to cook,' said Rodney. 'And no tinned baked beans please.'

Sara went upstairs to the front bedroom, dumped her knapsack on the floor, took off her socks and shorts and sat on one of the beds. She remembered the sandwich she had packed, but not eaten. She took it out of the knapsack, poured coffee from the thermos and ate and drank. She would lie on the bed – just for a moment, she thought – before starting dinner. She lay down. She fell into deep sleep.

When Sara woke it was light, the bright light of late morning. The bed next to her was empty. She padded across to the window, drew back the curtains and looked out. Veronica lay in a bikini on Sara's lilo on the lawn; Rodney was rubbing sun tan lotion on her back. Peter and John were playing French cricket with Sara's tennis racquet. Carla and Nick were sitting on the grass, languidly tossing Sara's frisbee to and fro. The Hound was chewing one of Sara's flippers.

She looked at her watch. It was after ten o'clock. She dressed hurriedly, made herself a snack, took the bike and wheeled it round the corner of the cottage into the front garden. 'Well, look who's here,' said Nick. 'The original sleeping beauty,' said John, 'only she didn't have a prince to wake her.' Rodney said, 'We've put you down for dinner, seeing as you chickened out again last night.' Sara said nothing. She mounted the bike and set off.

She freewheeled into the village, pedalled doggedly through it, then tackled the hill on the other side. The sun was hot. Sweat dripped into her eyes. She turned up a lane which was even steeper than the road she had just left. She pressed on, walking when she was forced to until – she checked her watch – it was one o'clock. The morning was over. She stopped and sat on the grass verge. Far below, the sea sparkled under a shimmering haze of heat. Tiny boats bobbed in the harbour. She stretched her aching legs. What should she do now?

She climbed onto the bike and set off in the direction from which she had come, gathering speed as she descended. She went faster and faster, swinging round corners, bumping over uneven patches in the lane. At the junction with the road she braked just long enough to see that nothing was coming then turned right and careered wildly down the long hill into the village.

She decided to take a look at the harbour. She pushed the bike along the quay, sniffing the tarry, fishy air. The tide was in; water lapped against the harbour wall. She came to a blackboard on which she read, 'Sea fishing. Two p.m. Ten pounds.' Sea fishing! That's what she would do next. She groped in the pocket of her shorts. She had just enough money.

There were two other passengers in the boat. Sara ignored them as the boat chugged out to sea; soon the harbour and the cliffs were a long way away. The boat stopped and its owner announced, 'We'll try here. Take a rod each.' Sara dropped her line into the water and let it unravel. Time drifted past. Suddenly her line tightened, so suddenly she squeaked with surprise. 'You've caught one,' said the boat owner, 'reel in your line.' Sara reeled. The pull of the invisible creature grew stronger. Now she could see shapes beneath the water; now there were three, no here came another one — four — silvery fish dancing in mid-air on her line. Icy drops of water fell from them onto her sun-warmed arms. The mackerel landed slithering on the deck. The boat owner seized them, twisted the hooks from their mouths and tossed the fish, tails still flapping, into a bucket. 'Quick, reel your line out again,' he said, as one of the other two people squealed, 'I've caught one.'

Soon all three of them were reeling out and reeling in, pouncing on the fish as soon as they could reach them and pulling the hooks from their mouths. The air was filled with wriggling fish and bright drops of water. Sara's arms ached from the weight of the rod and the reel. The bucket seethed with dying fish. Blood from their mouths stained the deck. 'Time to stop and turn back,' said the boat owner.

She carried her haul up the hill to the cottage where she found the kitchen empty once again, although she could hear people talking in the living room. She tipped the fish into the sink and began to clean them. She planned to grill them until their skins were brown and crackly. She would eat hers with mustard, a green salad and French bread. Fresh fruit afterwards with cheese. Simple, quick, delicious. She could hardly wait.

The door to the living room opened and Rodney came in. 'What's that wonderful smell?' He pulled out the grill. 'Mackerel! Terrific idea. I'll bet they're really fresh. Probably caught last night.' He pushed them back under the heat.

'I caught them. This afternoon.'

'You what? You caught them? How?'

'I went in a boat. Miles out to sea. It cost ten pounds.'

He strode back to the living room doorway. 'Hey, everyone,' he announced, 'you'll never believe what Sara's done, the trouble she's taken over dinner.' He turned back to her. 'What are we having with them?'

She told him. 'Not bad. Not bad at all,' he judged. 'Mind you, if you'd said in advance I would have done gooseberry sauce. And new potatoes. That would have lifted the meal into the gourmet class.'

'You're not on the rota for cooking.'

'I'll check who is.' He crossed the room and consulted the list on the wall. 'John,' he said. 'Incidentally, according to this we're both down for beds tonight. We can have the room you chose at the beginning of the week.'

'I don't need any help with the food. John can lay the table.'

'I'll tell him to get his skates on. And I'll ask Nick and Peter about which wine.'

The kitchen became a hive of activity. Nick and Peter were standing in front of the fridge arguing over whether a Muscadet or a white Burgundy would best bring out the flavour of the fish. Rodney was discussing with Veronica whether people should be given the choice of English or French mustard. John was setting out knives and forks. Carla was arranging a posy of wild flowers for the centre of the table. And The Hound was rushing about sniffing and getting under everyone's feet.

In just over ten minutes they all sat down. And oh, they were impressed! Between mouthfuls they exclaimed at

Sara's cleverness and at the tastiness of the fish. Sara did not reply; she was too hungry to spare any attention from her food. As soon as they finished the first course Rodney raised his wine glass. 'A toast to Sara,' he proposed, 'for the best meal yet.' 'To Sara,' echoed the others, 'for the best meal.'

There was a pause. 'You're supposed to respond,' Rodney prompted.

Sara placed her knife and fork neatly on her plate and turned to Peter. 'Peter,' she said, 'you and John. This morning you were playing French cricket with my tennis racquet which I have just had restrung.'

'Carla,' she looked at Carla. 'You used my cards yesterday and now the three of hearts is missing.'

'Nick,' she faced him. 'You were playing with my frisbee. And your dog has chewed one of my flippers.'

'Veronica,' she went on. 'You were lying on my lilo this morning. While Rodney was oiling your back.'

There was another pause. 'We thought you wouldn't mind,' said Rodney.

John said quickly, 'What would people like to play after dinner? There's this game I wanted to teach everyone.'

'Let Sara choose.' Rodney picked up a not-quite empty bottle of Muscadet. 'There's a drop left in here.' He leaned towards her. She placed the flat of her hand over her glass as he tried to pour.

'Of course I don't mind.' She smiled, turning her head first to one side, then to the other so that they could all see the smile. 'You are very welcome to use my things. Don't feel you have to ask. Just go ahead. Assume it's okay,' and she rose from the table and went upstairs. She did not go to the room with the twin beds but to the single room with the sloping ceiling. She undressed and climbed stiffly into bed. Only two days left, she thought, as she lay in the dark. Tomorrow she would book another ride; she would fit in a swim before breakfast, possibly before dinner as well; and the day after that she would walk – thirty miles would be a reasonable target this time. She fell asleep.

It was Saturday and Sara and Rodney had finished packing. The others had left. The cottage was locked up. 'Well,' said Rodney as he opened the car door. 'Terrific idea of mine inviting people, wasn't it? Everyone loved the ratatouille. And the stuffed artichoke hearts. Pity I didn't have time to make bouillabaisse. Still, it was the best week yet. In my book anyway.'

Sara said, 'The riding was something else. And I couldn't have done without the bike. Only trouble was I had so much to do; I never even had a chance to snorkel. Or to start the Zoë Oldenburg. I didn't have a moment to spare.'

'Me neither. Roll on next year.'

THE PERFECT MAN

Maggie spent the early part of the evening putting together her persona – scarlet lipstick and nail varnish, pale face, sheer black tights, a brief black dress with a bustier top, a black cloche hat, flat lace-up boots, long green earrings and finally a huge, spiky, green cat brooch pinned to her belt.

The result was all she intended – glamorous, enticing, unusual. She would do her hosts credit. Yet when she arrived, when she knocked at the door and waited outside, bits of the outfit threatened to dissociate, to turn ugly and risible. The cat brooch stuck out; the bustier was precarious; worse, she could see the tips of her toes so her shoulders must have rounded, her head drooped.

'Maggie!' Roger exclaimed when he opened the door. 'You look great. That cat is magic. How do you find these things?' Everything she was wearing shot into line. 'Come and have a drink,' he added.

He led her through the crowded flat to the kitchen and poured her a glass of wine. 'You have to meet Tony,' he said. He propelled her into the living room towards a fair man. 'Tony, I don't think you know Maggie,' he said to the man. 'She lives next door.'

Maggie looked at Tony. 'Means I don't have to drive

home at any rate,' she said. 'Did you come by car?'

'Yes. Brought a couple of other people.'

Conversation was easy after that; she questioned Tony on the make, model and year of his car. She progressed to a range of general likes and dislikes, favourite foods, politics and leisure pursuits. But it was not so easy to brush him off afterwards. She managed to escape to the kitchen on the pretext of having seen an old friend heading in that direction.

'Any joy?' Caroline, Roger's partner, came into the kitchen to refill a couple of glasses.

'Afraid not, sorry. His ears are huge. He smokes a pipe. He drives a Mini Metro.'

'Have to try again later,' said Caroline, leaving to answer the front door.

'Shouldn't a familiar sit on the shoulder rather than the waist?' suggested a new voice behind Maggie.

She turned and was relieved to see someone who bore absolutely no resemblance to the man she had described to Roger and Caroline. She had specified fair hair, slim build, regular features, smooth skin. Nothing like the man who had spoken about her cat brooch.

She had no idea who he was. She didn't ask his name she preferred to guess. Not Jeremy or Simon – too Channel Four. Not Chris – too lighweight. Fred was too mundane. Something a bit primitive perhaps – mythical or Biblical. Jason? Matthew? No, Luke was the one.

'I'm wondering what to eat first,' Maggie said.

'Is it safe?' His blue eyes widened with the question.

'Safe? What on earth do you mean? Caroline and Roger make absolutely everything themselves. Even the bread.'

'Can I be sure you won't slip a charm or something worse into the humous. I think I'll just watch.'

'Oh Lord, there's Godfrey,' she said.

Godfrey always complained about her though they split up a year ago. He was doing it again. 'I mean,' he was saying to Caroline, 'she'd bring something to the table and I'd have to ask what it was. I'd never seen anything like it before. She'd claim it was quite ordinary – fish cakes, only they went wrong – that sort of thing. She even made pound cake – you know, a pound of butter, a pound of flour, a pound of eggs – without weighing anything.'

Maggie approached Godfrey and said over his shoulder, 'I made it by the pound cake method. You cream the butter first, add the egg yolks, then the whites whipped separately, then the flour.'

Luke had disappeared while she was talking to Godfrey. Roger arrived at her elbow with more wine and a further introduction. This man looked promising. Crisp hair curling on his collar, Levi 501s and a taupe cotton shirt. By the look of him he might well have left a genuine World War Two leather bomber jacket in the bedroom. But did he like hats? she decided to ask.

'Forties cloches like yours, yes. I can't abide those Afghan caps everyone is wearing now.'

'What about shoes?'

'I like your little pointed boots.'

'Hardly little at six and a half, or whatever that is in metric. I still can't convert in my head.'

'Second nature to me. I spend a great deal of my time in the Community; Brussels and Luxembourg for the most part. To my mind the yard, foot and inch are as antiquated as the rod, pole and perch.'

'Oh, there's Laura in the other room' Maggie waved cheerily to a woman she did not know. 'I must say hello. Catch you later.'

She threaded her way purposefully between people. Caroline turned from a conversation as Maggie passed and said in a conspiratorial whisper. 'What's the verdict on Jeremy?'

'He has no respect for the foot. And he talks like a translation.'

Roger, who was always in charge of the music, had decided the party was ready for nostalgia – the 60s by the sound of it – someone, Maggie couldn't remember who, was singing a song called 'Hats off to Larry'.

Luke reappeared. 'Do you like hats?' Maggie asked him.

'Is yours an attempt at disguise?' His face creased into a smile. 'Shall we try to reach the food again?'

'As long as I don't have to go past Godfrey.'

They headed back to the kitchen. Roger approached her with another tall, fair man. I'll come back later,' Maggie smiled at him.

Luke and Maggie found plenty of food. Salads, quiches, baked potatoes, cheese and bread covered the table; bowls of taramosalata, smoked mackerel pâté and humous stood on the worktops; a casserole simmered on the stove. Maggie crossed the room, lifted the lid of the pot and sniffed at the contents. 'What do you think this is?' she asked Luke. But the voice that replied was Godfrey's. Was he following her? 'Caroline told me it was cassoulet,' he announced. 'If you'd made it you'd presumably insist it was Irish stew. Or Lancashire hot pot.' He shrugged and made for the door.

'Oh dear,' Maggie turned to Luke. 'He makes me feel as though I ought to go and write "I must always measure my ingredients" five hundred times.'

Luke didn't say anything. But Roger, coming into the kitchen as Godfrey left, said, 'Might get it out of your system.' He picked up a corkscrew and began to open a bottle of wine. 'You know, you were quite different when you were with Godfrey.'

Caroline arrived. 'Could you open another one, Roger?' she asked, 'I'm doing the rounds.'

Maggie said to Roger. 'Godfrey didn't like it if I talked

too much. And he said the things I said were silly. Though when we were on our own he found some of them quite funny.'

'We all know Godfrey wasn't right for you.' That was Caroline's opinion. 'You deserve someone much better. Stop lurking in the kitchen and come and meet people.'

Maggie was about to protest that talking to Roger and Luke did not qualify as lurking, but Roger made off with a bottle in each hand and Luke had vanished again.

Caroline led Maggie back into the living room where she introduced Colin. 'I find it hard to know what to say to people,' Colin said straightaway. Maggie knew that if she felt like that she'd never say so. Men did though, even men who professed to be shy. Colin suggested they go into the next room to dance; she agreed.

'I'm not crackers,' she thought she heard him say next, through high-volume Madonna.

'What?'

'I've got crackers. In the bedroom. I wasn't sure about them once I arrived. Is it the right sort of party?'

'Why not?'

Among the coats in the bedroom was a leather bomber jacket which did look as though it could be genuine World War Two. Colin dug out a huge carrier bag. Not only crackers in it, but party hats and balloons.

Maggie blew up two balloons and handed them to Colin. 'Give these to the first person you come across, introduce yourself and see what happens,' she advised him, then set off on her own to the kitchen.

She inspected the food again; the baked potatoes were all gone; so was the cassoulet.

'I've brought your hat.' It was Luke. He was carrying a witch's hat. It must have come from Colin's collection.

'Did you come by car?' she asked Luke.

'What?'

'Car. What car do you drive?'

'I don't have a car.'

'You don't have a car.'

'No. Why do you keep rushing from room to room?'

He was smiling again, so there could be no harm in telling him. 'As long as you don't tell Roger or Caroline,' she warned.

'Not much choice, have I? If I tried I suspect I'd find I couldn't articulate the words. Or I might contract warts. Bubonic plague if you were really put out.'

'I'm escaping from them. They keep producing men.' She looked at Luke. He was leaning against the sink and listening to what she said. It wasn't the way party dialogues were supposed to go.

'I'm to blame,' she went on. 'After I split up with Godfrey they went on and on about how I should find someone else. In the end, to put them off, I told them I was quite clear about the type who attracted me and that there was no point in introducing me to anyone who didn't match up. Then I made the description so precise I would always find some reason to reject each and every candidate. I mean, really precise. Not just appearance, but habits, hobbies, lifestyle – the lot. Even the kind of car he drove. Now they complain I'm too fussy. But at least they believe I'm looking. And I am, honestly.'

'To keep Roger and Caroline happy? There must be easier ways.'

'Not without upsetting them.'

'You're the one with the power.'

Maggie was about to tell him not to talk nonsense when Caroline arrived, clasping a man's elbow in her right hand. 'Simon has been asking to meet you all evening,' she told Maggie.

Maggie looked at the man. And oh dear! On the surface this one fitted the bill exactly. The features, colouring and build were correct. The hair was exceptional, lightly-gelled with one designer curl sculpted on the brow. And the style was impeccable – Next trousers, a white shirt under a Fair Isle sweater. She turned in search of Luke but he must have taken off at Caroline's approach.

'Maggie's our next-door neighbour,' Caroline told Simon and left the two of them together.

'I love your boots,' Simon said. Maggie's brooch, her dress, her cloche, came in for similar praise. She began to ask Simon her usual questions and found that he drove a Merc, preferred cacti to ferns and voted Labour but only because there was no alternative. Purcell, Vivaldi and Telemann were among his favourite classical composers. William Morris prints, pre-Raphaelite paintings and Romantic poets left him cold, although Keats, especially in 'The Eve of St Agnes', had some good moments. Of contemporary writers Anthony Burgess was dazzling, Iris Murdoch dispassionate, Peter De Vries came close but John Updike hit the exact note. Maggie felt symptoms of panic: prickling facial heat, intermittent interference with her hearing. Why on earth had she been so precise in depicting her supposed ideal man to Caroline and Roger?

She heard that his flat, to which she foresaw she would soon be invited, was a mixture of Victorian (the furniture) and deco (the mirrors, the glass). He hated all soaps, especially *Neighbours*. He did a great deal of walking. He played tennis. He didn't jog. He rarely ate red meat. This was terrible; he was exactly as she had envisaged. What could she do?

Caroline returned, 'Everything all right?' and offered them both more wine.

Maggie looked desperately around the room. She was small and cold. She ought to have worn high heels. And a jacket. Could she feel sick. Or hungry, which she was. Could she make an excuse and run?

She felt a tap on her shoulder. 'I assume this is yours.' Luke handed her a broom. 'I found it in the kitchen cupboard. You'll need it if you're going to take off.'

Simon said, 'I haven't eaten yet. Have you?'

Maggie leant the broom against the wall. She didn't like to leave it there; someone might fall over it. But she had no choice. She would look odd carrying it around.

'No, I haven't Simon,' she replied. 'But I'm just going to the loo. I won't be a moment.'

Once there, in a temporary safe place, she sat down, took a pen from her bag and wrote in a page of her diary 'Means of Escape'. Writing things down always clarified her thoughts.

She wrote a list.

1. I have flu symptoms.
2. I feel sick.
3. I've left the iron/oven/electric fire on.
4. I have to get up at 5.30 tomorrow to fly to Manchester to interview a woman who collects bassoons.
5. I do volunteer work for a victim support scheme. My telephone duty starts in ten minutes.

Someone tried the door. 'Out in a minute,' she said in a bright, encouraging tone.

6. I work nights – in a news bureau, as a croupier in a nightclub, as a waitress.

The door shook. Maggie stood up, shot the bolt and let herself out. 'Sorry,' she muttered.

A pity Simon hadn't stayed in the kitchen. He was lying in wait in the hallway, where he was impossible to overlook, forking salad into his well-shaped mouth. A frond of endive approached his lips, hovered, was gripped firmly by admirably white teeth. He bit through the frond; half of it fell onto the floor. Too late she regretted that her blueprint contained no clause on messy eating.

He said, 'Oh there you are. Good.'

Roger appeared, paused, said quietly to Maggie, 'So glad to see you two have got together,' and then took off again.

'I brought you the best of what was left,' Simon went on. He turned, took a plate of food from the hall table and offered it, making sure his hand just grazed hers in the passing.

She saw splinters of bright, sharp, angry light. She looked from the plate up at Simon and a spark struck his eyes. Another landed on his cheek where it sizzled and went out. She looked back down at her hand holding the plate. Her nails had grown longer, dangerous. She heard a hissing sound.

She looked up again and saw Simon's eyes were shrinking, his gaze shifting, avoiding hers. His cheeks grew puffy. 'If you're free next week, we could perhaps see the new Cher film,' he suggested, as if unaware.

Of course she was free. He was no ideal man now.

'About time,' the voice was Luke's. 'What about the others?'

Maggie said, 'See you later, Simon. See you later, Luke,' and set off.

No problem to find the World War Two hero – owner of the bomber jacket – and to change the colour of his trousers to turquoise at a glance. She found large-eared Tony and made his ears larger. She roamed the room. Tall, fair men gazed into her eyes and were transformed. She adjusted a nose here, a thigh there, she shifted the alignment of a particularly alluring set of eyebrows, unzipped flies to inspect their contents, was disappointed and failed to put them back back properly, so they peeked, pinkly, from between metal teeth.

Time to make enquiries. She found Roger. 'Have you seen Luke anywhere?'

'Luke who?'

'Guy with black hair and blue eyes. Don't know his last name. He brought me a broomstick. It's leaning against the wall.'

'How much have you had to drink, Maggie?'

'You must know him,' she persisted. 'Lots of lines on his face. Wearing a black sweater and rather old black jeans.'

'Hand on heart, no.'

'You saw him with me earlier. We were in the kitchen together when Caroline said I should meet Colin.'

Roger looked at her oddly. 'You weren't with anyone in the kitchen. That's why Caroline wanted you to go and meet people. Look, why don't you have a chat with Philip? He's just your type. And he's another one who's been admiring you from afar.' Roger started to propel her in the direction of yet another tall, fair man.

'Thanks, Roger, but I have to look for someone.'

The broom was no longer against the wall, though that was not conclusive. Someone could have put it away or be using it to sweep up a broken wine glass. But when she went into the kitchen there was no sign of the witch's hat. She went over the sequence of events in her mind. Luke had come into the kitchen with the hat. He had offered it to her. She had not taken it. He had put it on the draining board. So where was it now?

Caroline entered the room, followed by Godfrey. 'Caroline, thank goodness you've turned up,' said Maggie. 'Roger says he didn't see me with anyone in the kitchen earlier. Before you introduced me to Colin. I was with someone, wasn't I? Dark man with blue eyes. Holding a witch's hat.'

'A man in a witch's hat! She's gone over the top. I knew it would happen. Drunk as a newt,' said Godfrey.

'You were on your own, Maggie,' said Caroline. 'Looking at the food.'

'No you weren't,' said Luke. She looked round, but Caroline was right. There was no one there. She ought to have guessed.

'Of course I was. Yes. Sorry,' she said quickly. 'It was only a joke.' Godfrey didn't laugh and Caroline said. 'I don't see how it was meant to be funny. What happened to Simon?'

'We didn't get on.'

'What a pity. How about Chris? Over there.'

'No,' said Maggie. She poured more wine and took a sip. 'The person I want to meet is . . .' She looked about the kitchen, walked to the doorway, looked around the living room and turned back to Caroline. 'That man by the window. The one with the slouch hat. Looks like Lou Grant.'

'But he's fat!' said Caroline. 'And short. He wears the hat because he's bald!'

'That's nothing to do with anything. He looks interesting.' Maggie paused. 'On second thoughts,' she said, 'I'll introduce myself,' and set off across the room. Before she left the party, she must look for the witch's hat.

PESTS

How that princess ever managed to kiss a frog is beyond me. For a start, frogs and toads, they both jump. If you were to approach one, ever so cautious, lips pursed for the coming osculation, it would leap, trailing warty legs. It might jump away from you or – horror – towards you. In principle, in any case, the story of the princess and the frog is unacceptable. Not that I have anything against ugliness. Some of the most attractive men are ugly. No; it is the idea that if you force yourself to offer sexual favours to an abhorrent creature you will be rewarded by its transformation into a beautiful prince.

I have always found frogs and toads abhorrent. I made no secret of this when me and my ex were on good terms. I insisted that toads, in particular, were malicious. I knew it by the way their eyes glowed green and yellow in the dark and because they always hopped in my direction in spite of how much I hated them.

Proof of their evil intentions came the day the dog caught one. The dog played with it, as dogs will, nose to the ground between his paws, retreating to full height with a sharp bark, rolling the toad over to expose its horrible pale underside. For other prey, a rat for instance, death would be next. But the dog, toad between teeth, jaws primed to gnash, began to foam, in spurts, like a washing machine, and dropped the beast on its uneven back leaving me to confront the hideous creature putting itself to rights.

The dog is long since gone, though not, so far as I know, as a result of its encounter with the toad. My ex is now my ex. I live alone with my garden, a patch of London land which I have reclaimed from waist-high thistles, elderberries, brambles and rose thorns to a restrained wilderness of my own design.

My garden is all the more attractive because the gardens on either side are so rampant and untended: places where moss covers the paths, the grass is yellow and long and the stalks of sycamore seedlings have red, fungoid lumps.

By attractive, I mean my garden attracts everything. The first year after I moved in I found snails, morning after morning, an infantry of them, silvering across the damp lawn. A host of them slid onto my lupins, waving their horns and munching. The lupins died. I dissolved the snails with slug pellets. Soon, empty shells lay everywhere.

During the second summer, the ants came. They nested under my lawn and the nest made a bulge in the smooth green turf. I studied my gardening books. Following the instructions, I filled my saucepans and kettle with water and set them all to boil. I went into the garden where I made an H-shaped cut through to the nest with a spade. It took courage to do this as I was fearful the ants might swarm over the spade and run all the way up the handle to my hands. After I made the cut I folded back the turf (still using the spade) and saw the nest. Thousands and thousands of ants seethed in it. I quickly poured the kettle full of water over them, then the contents of all four saucepans. It wasn't enough. I ran to and fro from the kitchen for some time with saucepans and kettles of boiling water. Even when all sign of life had gone I kept on feeling itchy. I replaced the portion of turf, reseeded its damaged edges with ryegrass mix and within weeks the site of the ants' nest was again as smooth and green as the rest of the lawn.

I can't remember all the other pests in my garden, there have been so many. At one time there were silver-winged ants. Then wasps; a cloud of them hovered around my Virginia creeper where I suspected they had a nest. I called the local council who told me the wasps were best left until the end of the season when they would follow their queen and find somewhere else to live. The third summer I came across greenflies which I easily killed with Melathion. The black fly were more tenacious, clinging beneath the elderberry leaves and disfiguring the stalks of the nicotania; but I killed them too eventually – regular doses of poison dust did the trick.

The garden became orderly. A smooth green carpet lay at its centre. In the shady spots flourished hostas, and in the full sun, nasturtiums, clarkias, stocks and geraniums bloomed. Tomatoes leaned on stakes, runner beans twined round a wigwam of canes and rambling roses rambled over their appointed places.

Last year the pests were replaced by harmless, pretty creatures who loved my city oasis of colour and scent. Bees – the bumble and the honey – and butterflies – red admirals and small, delicate blue ones whose name I did not know – tilted at each other in the warm summer air. Fat grey pigeons and speckled thrushes bent the branches of the elderberries in the autumn, pecked at the fruit and flapped into the sky when frightened by my cat.

My cat is a large tabby tom. He works for me, although the work is self-imposed. He works as an odd-job man or possibly, given the nature of the work, as a husband. He brings things home. Sometimes something relatively innocent such as a chewed sausage or a chicken bone, or a scrap of toast with a little fish paste sticking to it.

Sometimes something more offensive. An almost-dead thrush in the living room, feathers scattered, entrails on show, wings still twitching: and a severed claw in the hall. A stiff rat in the passage, over which he meows his triumph. When I go on holiday he slaughters a whole nestful of starlings to celebrate my return, spreads embryos and eggs all over the carpet, across the sofa and under the bed. Then he vomits among his trophies.

Of course I hate cleaning all this up, but he means well. And many of the objects my ex used to bring home were equally unwelcome and led to as much mess. Other women, for instance.

This summer I went to Spain: on my own as usual. The holiday was a hot interlude beneath a blue sky beside a blue pool. I chose a spot well away from the wasp-infested rubbish bins and kept my eyes on my book when the shadow of a man cast over it. I had cool water to splash in, a cool shower in the evening and enough crisp, cotton clothes to change in and out of without once washing a thing.

When I returned to my flat the cat meowed a welcome and rubbed himself against my legs. In the living room I found the usual debris. I took off my jacket and set about clearing up dead birds. I carried the mess, in the dustpan, into the garden.

While I was away it must have rained. Everything was lush; the lawn needed mowing; the geraniums needed dead-heading; the runner beans needed picking. Also I spotted traces of snails. I approached the compost heap and saw a small cloud of whiteflies rise from it. Tomorrow I would find chemical solutions to these new problems. I tipped the remains of the birds into the compost. Something moved against my sandalled foot. I looked down. I thought it was a brown leaf, but it moved again, and I saw the object of my greatest dread, a toad. I dropped the dustpan and ran indoors.

The next day, although I sprayed the pests, as I knew I must, I stood at arm's length from the compost heap and wore jeans and high-rise trainers. Afterwards I skirted that corner of the garden and let the weeds grow. It was my offering. I hoped to placate the toad.

My ex and I still met every six months or so, I don't know why. These occasions, so far as I could tell, brought neither of us any pleasure. But we both tried hard.

Before the summer faded it was time, once more, for us to get together. It was his turn to visit me. I took him into my garden. We always showed each other what we achieved.

He looked at the springy, sharp-edged lawn, the borders of stocks and pansies backed by honeysuckle and late roses, the baskets of purple trailing lobelias, red geraniums and white alyssum hanging on the walls.

We walked past the beans and the tomatoes. I turned to go back.

'What's that bit?' he asked, pointing to the small area I had left to the toad.

I explained. 'You know I've always hated toads.'

'There can't have been a toad. You imagined it,' he said.

That night I dreamed of the toad I had imagined. He invaded the bedroom and hopped, scabrous, all over me while I lay there, unable to move. He became vast and covered me, covered my face, his hideous throat working. I woke to find myself screaming and the cat standing on my chest.

On other nights I dreamed of other pests. Of spiders which squatted on the floor, then criss-crossed my face, hairily, of mice which scampered in the wardrobe and of lizards, steely blue and green.

In the daytimes I made the flat secure against all creatures. I replaced each plug – in the wash basin, the bath, the sink. I poured bleach down the loo. I nailed airtight strips around doors and windows. I glued up the cat flap. I sprayed the letter box with insect repellent. I abandoned the garden, which harboured the non-existent toad.

In the bathroom I saw silverfish. In the kitchen I scoured the cupboards, and poured disinfectant over small black creatures like woodlice. The creatures died on their backs in viscous green pools. I went shopping and filled an entire cupboard with the sprays and powders and liquids of chemical death. I couldn't find anything in any of the shops to kill toads but reasoned that there was no way now for a toad to enter the flat. Besides, there was no toad.

I still could not relax. I called in the experts.

'And what is it this time?' said the man from the council. It was his third visit. The first was because I was sure the wasps had returned. The second was when I had mistaken a stag beetle for a cockroach.

'Rats,' I told him, but he opened the cover on the drain outside my back door and showed me the trap to stop rats climbing up. Did that mean they were lurking, massed behind the trap, below the surface, in angry, diseased hordes? I didn't dare ask.

Every week, for one reason or another, there was a man about the place, looking for some creature I'd seen, or thought I'd seen. They were all men. It was dick-work, routing out pests, for which I paid a fair price.

After these visits, I slept the whole night. Slept the whole night several nights. Became confident and prised the cat flap open again.

That night the dream returned. Things crept across the room, then hovered above me, pale and threatening to suffocate me. Small creatures poured into the room, from under the door, screaming. I woke. I realised slowly that the screams were coming from the kitchen.

I switched on the light in the bedroom. I switched on the light in the hall. I stepped forward and switched on the light in the kitchen. I saw the cat; the cat was crouched over some creature. I switched off the light and closed the kitchen door quickly, thankful for the seal I had fixed under it. And although I could still hear the screams and although they were real and terrible I slept well and late.

In the morning I opened the kitchen door an inch or two and peered inside. The cat rushed past me into the hallway. Then I spotted something small, black and misshapen at the other end of the kitchen. I looked at it. It lay still. It was dead. I took a step forward. It heaved. I slammed the kitchen door, kicked the cat with my bare foot, rushed into the bedroom and flung open the window to let him run out.

I peered into the kitchen again. The creature did not heave. But it was in a different place! I slammed the door again.

I called 'Quick Kill' because this was no job for the council; it was an emergency. The woman I spoke to on the phone realised this immediately and within the hour a man in a boiler suit arrived.

'In there,' I said, pointing to the closed kitchen door. He opened it; I stood in the doorway while he approached the creature.

'It's a frog,' he said, bending over it. But I knew it was the toad.

'It's dead.' He picked it up by one long back leg. He carried the dead toad into the overgrown garden. I directed him to the corner where I knew the compost heap was. I could not see the heap; it was hidden by brambles nowadays.

He deposited the toad and we returned indoors. 'Thank you for coming so quickly,' I said to the man as I wrote a cheque.

'Any time,' he responded. 'Next time you have a problem, just ring the office and ask for George. I work weekends too.'

The cat did not return until late afternoon. He curled his tail round my legs, rubbing his body against me. I loved him too, with reservations. While he was out I had rewritten my will so that I left nothing to my ex. I had decided to leave everything in trust to the cat.

Tomorrow I would take my new will to my solicitor. Not that I planned on dying. I would kill them all first.

WHAT BECAME OF JENNY

One Saturday, shortly before 3.47 p.m., Jenny's car exploded. Jenny was in the car at the time, in the Liverpool Road, London N1, making a right turn at the traffic lights into Islington Park Street.

The light was green when she reached it. She halted, set her indicator flashing, and waited, drumming her fingers on the leather steering wheel. The light turned red; a lorry travelling in the opposite direction stopped. The man in the cab smiled down at Jenny and waved her on. She raised her hand in acknowledgment, turned right, passed under the nose of the lorry and her car exploded.

The force of the explosion flung Jenny against her seat belt and flung her car sideways, tyres screeching. Jenny heard metal tear. She watched the dashboard crumple into an inverted V, saw every light in front of her – oil, ignition, even the one in the radio – flash on, then off. The car rocked to a halt.

She sat still for a second, then thought fire might follow explosion as she had seen in films and climbed out quickly; broken glass crunched under her feet. 'Are you all right?' asked a voice. She turned, saw a dark, young man clambering from a red sports car and saw that the nose of the sports car was tucked into the offside door of her Mini. 'You're very pale,' he continued anxiously. She looked at her watch to see whether it had stopped too; but the seconds were flashing away and the time, she registered, was 3.47 p.m. 'I think I'm okay,' she replied slowly, 'but my car must be a write-off.'

'I'll ask one of those people to help me push it into the side,' the driver of the sports car went on. Jenny looked beyond him and discovered a small crowd of spectators teetering on the kerb. She watched two of them manhandle the Mini out of the way and wondered what would become of her without it.

Jenny was living with Brian when she decided to buy a car. 'But why?' he demanded, when she told him of her plan. 'You take the Tube to work. And I'll run you anywhere you want at weekends. Seeing as you can't drive the Beetle.'

'I can, except for double de-clutching.'

'I told you. Clutch down. Into neutral. Plenty of revs. Clutch down again. Into gear. Easy peasy.'

'It's the doors, as well,' Jenny went on. 'I can't be sure of being able to open them since the hinges dropped. Remember when I had to catch a bus home to fetch you? Suppose I'd been inside the car?'

'I said I'll drive. Besides where is it you so desperately want to go?'

'Brian, the Beetle just isn't reliable.'

'It always gets me from A to B.'

Jenny stopped arguing; she knew she wouldn't win. Instead she would pursue her plan.

A few days later she spotted an ad in the *Standard* for a Mini at just the right price. She phoned and arranged to see the car. She saw it and held her breath. She saw a shiny, Inca yellow Clubman without a single dent or scratch: with a black vinyl top, a black stripe along the side, nudge bars and fog lamps. She let out her breath in a rush. She opened the driver's door: it opened easily. She sat in the seat: the seat was cloth, not plastic, the steering wheel was leather-covered, the dashboard was of walnut. Below the dashboard was a radio cassette. Jenny looked behind her; there were two speakers on the empty back shelf. She could listen to music as she drove.

She switched on the ignition and the engine started straight away, nothing rattled. The clutch slipped in smoothly. She released the handbrake and the car leapt forward. She drove it through the tricky, narrow streets of Hampstead with mounting excitement, then down Swains Lane, east into Chester Road and finally up Highgate Hill. The car took the hill easily. She stopped at the traffic lights on the steepest part; the handbrake held. She bought the car.

'Good God,' said Brian when she arrived home in it. 'It's a yob's car. Are you going to hang furry dice in the front window? Or sit a nodding dog on the back shelf?'

On Monday morning Brian set off for work as usual, but returned in a few minutes. 'The Beetle won't start,' he announced. 'I'll have to take your new one.'

'I thought you said it was a yob's car.'

'Beggars can't be choosers. Can I have the keys?'

Jenny tried to think of a reason why he couldn't, but there wasn't one. 'I'd better show you how the gears work,' she suggested, but Brian replied, 'Don't be ridiculous. Anyone can drive a Mini,' and left.

For the rest of the week he didn't try the Beetle; he took Jenny's car instead. On Saturday morning, while he was out collecting subs for the Labour Party, Jenny packed three suitcases and a box of cassettes, wrote a note saying she'd be back for her books and plants and slipped into her car. She discovered her feet could not reach the pedals; Brian had adjusted the seat to accommodate his much longer legs. She adjusted it to fit hers and drove away.

After a short period of flat-hunting and sleeping on friends' floors, Jenny found a place to rent in Hackney which she supposed would do for now. She looked round it with some disdain. It was 'furnished' with a rickety bed, an old chest of drawers (the bedroom), a wobbly, formica-topped table, two upright chairs, a threadbare rug, a gas heater and several wooden cupboards (the living room). It was miles from the Tube and was above an off-licence in a tatty modern block, in a dodgy-looking area. But it was cheap; Jenny would drive to work, she decided; she would spend most of her evenings out; and once she was inside the car, with both doors locked, she would be quite safe.

The journey to work soon became a pleasure. Jenny took pride in her driving and pride, too, in her courtesy. She rarely hooted at other drivers; instead she made eye contact, smiled and gave way with good grace. Cabbies smiled back and made room for her. Bus drivers gave her the thumbs-up to thank her for letting them pull out. Men in delivery vans gestured politely for her to go first.

She took pride, too, in knowing her way about. She studied the large scale *London Geographia* to find the shortest, least-congested routes. She listened to the car radio; when it said Arsenal were playing at home she avoided Holloway, when it announced there was a State visit she stayed out of Whitehall, when it warned of a 'Troops Out' march she gave Islington a miss.

In the evenings she drove round her neighbourhood – just for the fun of it. She whizzed up Mare Street and round the one-way system with The Eagles on tape and roared along the Ball's Pond Road listening to Prince. At weekends she went further afield, tearing through narrow empty lanes in the Chilterns with a Sting tape playing; zooming up the A12 to the sound of Springsteen; whirling round the M25 with Robert Palmer at full volume. She went faster and faster, grew more and more skilled at cornering, even at double de-clutching. And she felt as though she were flying.

One afternoon, in a deserted country road, a dishevelled man tried to flag her down, then stepped right out into the road in front of her; but she swerved swiftly round him and sped away. One night, late, when she stopped at a red light in Tottenham, a youth left the pavement, approached the car and tapped on her window, mumbling; but Jenny eased in the clutch, released the handbrake, the light turned amber and she was off. And one evening, after work, she returned to Hackney to find Brian standing under the broken street lamp outside the off-licence.

She climbed out of the car. 'Can we talk?' he asked. 'I suppose you'd better come in,' she replied, unlocked her door and led him upstairs to the flat.

She ushered him into the living room. 'I'm afraid you'll have to sit on an upright chair,' she apologised. 'I'm afraid I've only coffee to drink.'

'I'd prefer a glass of wine. I can pop downstairs and buy a bottle,' he suggested.

'Not for me, thanks. I'm driving.'

'Where to?' he asked. 'When?'

'Wherever,' said Jenny. 'Later on. Do you want coffee?'

'Okay.' Brian looked around. 'Not exactly cosy, this place, is it? How long are you planning to stay?'

'I haven't thought.' Jenny went into the kitchenette and plugged in the kettle.

'I mean, how soon are you coming back? Tonight? Next week? Or when? It's ridiculous you living like this. You've made your point.'

'How's the Beetle,' Jenny asked him, 'Still in action?'

'The what? Oh, the car. It died. Towed away for scrap.'

'How did you come here tonight?'

'I had to take a bus,' he complained, 'but we can go home in yours.' Jenny unplugged the kettle and told him, 'I'll give you a lift because it's on my way. Then I'm off somewhere else.' She looked at her watch. 'We'll have to go now or I'll be late.'

He followed her downstairs, she let him into the car and settled into the driving seat. In theory, Jenny thought, as she tried to release the handbrake without brushing against Brian's leg, there was room in the Mini, not just for Jenny and Brian, but for Jenny and Brian and two other people. She shivered with claustrophobia at the thought. She drove quickly to Kentish Town, reached the end of Brian's road, stopped and said, 'I'll have to drop you here. Sorry about the rush.' She waited, staring stonily ahead, until he left.

She locked the passenger door behind him, breathed a sigh of relief and made a U turn. She inserted a David Bowie tape in the deck, but it sounded far too loud. She switched it off. Even without Brian the car felt small now. She drove back to Hackney and parked. She took two pairs of gloves, a screwdriver, a tin of boiled sweets and a handful of biros from the glove compartment. She took a can of anti-freeze, a stack of tapes, a silk scarf, a pair of trainers, an empty Tupperware box and a column of paper cups from the side pockets. She carried everything upstairs to her flat and set it all on the formica-topped table. She looked around. At the very least she should buy a better table, she thought. And perhaps a picture or two for the walls?

On Saturday, as usual, she washed the car and waxed it and polished its chrome trim. She walked to the corner shop where she bought a bottle of Ajax to shine its windows. When she returned she found a long, dark scratch on the Mini's nearside wing; she would see the scratch every time she opened her door.

That evening Jenny did not drive around the streets. She bought a bottle of wine from the off-licence, went up to her living room, poured wine into a paper cup and sat on the floor listening to people going in and out of the shop below. The floor would be more comfortable to sit on, she thought, if she had a decent rug.

On Sunday morning she decided to take the car to Epping Forest. She went downstairs, opened the street door and stopped, shocked. Someone had stolen her fog lamps in the night. She hurried to the car, found the door had been forced and looked inside. The thief had also made off with the radio cassette and some tapes. She rang the police; two policemen turned up, shook their heads sadly, said there was really no way they could trace anything, asked her if she would like to talk to someone from the victim support scheme and went away again. Jenny didn't go to Epping Forest. The trip wouldn't be the same without music.

On Monday the car still felt small inside. Outside it didn't seem to be small enough. On the way to work Jenny made a dash for a gap in the traffic, misjudged the size of the gap, scraped a car on her offside and smashed its wing mirror. She stopped, climbed out and found a new, deep scratch on her own wing. The driver of the other car climbed out too and the words and gestures he and she exchanged were not courteous in the least.

On Tuesday evening Jenny went for a spin along the North Circular, was pursued by a police car, apprehended and cautioned for speeding. And the following Saturday the car exploded.

Jenny put in a claim to her insurance company. When the cheque arrived she spent an entire day shopping; she bought a solid pine table, a comfortable chair, two rather attractive water colours, a radio/cassette player, a pink and white striped rug and a copy each of *Motor Cycle News*, *Back Street Heroes*, *Superbike* and *Performance Bike*. That evening she slotted a Springsteen tape into the cassette player, settled in her chair and browsed through her new magazines.

A MONTH OF MINI CABS

'I hope this is going to work out,' Amy said. She and Max were lying side by side in the dark in his double bed. 'My being here, I mean.'

'Why shouldn't it?'

Well, thought Amy, for a start she had no idea how much he earned; she wasn't even sure exactly what he did – something connected with company formation he said, whatever that was. On some days he didn't seem to do anything. Had he inherited money? His clothes and furniture weren't over-the-top expensive, but neither were they shabby. His flat was lovely but – the thought suddenly struck her – he might not own it, might be a tenant; for all she knew he might be on housing benefit, income support, the dole. How could she begin to ask? She said, 'I'm not used to sharing a room.'

'No?'

'I mean it. The last person I shared a room with on a regular basis was my little sister Bridget. When we were kids.' She sat up sharply, pulling the covers with her and clasped her arms round her knees. 'I used to tell her stories in bed at night. They were really quite good.' Max said, 'Go to sleep.'

'Once upon a time,' Amy began, 'far in the future, there were no women in the world.'

'Don't start there,' Bridget objected. 'Start with the bubble.'

'That's not where it starts. It starts with Alasha being born: not born, coming out of the test tube. By mistake. I mean her being a girl was a mistake.'

'Start with the bubble,' Bridget repeated.

'Oh, all right. Once upon a time,' Amy began again, 'people had to wear bubbles as soon as they were old enough to walk. Alasha went to be fitted for hers when she was two.'

'I could walk before that,' Bridget said. 'I bet I could.'

'When she was one and a half, then. She went to a special room. It was a small room and it was painted white. A man measured Alasha, fetched a bubble and popped her inside.'

'Ow,' said Bridget softly because she knew what came next.

'Sh. The bubble was invented by a man called Josiah Tottle – I forgot to tell you that last time – who worked in a car factory. After he invented the bubble the car factory was pulled down and a bubble factory was built instead. He invented the bubble to stop people touching each other; because touching wasted time when people should be working or learning or inventing something else. You could see through your bubble; and you could reach outside it to shake hands or eat or write.'

'But you had to put your feet through the holes at the bottom and stand up straight and walk very carefully,' Bridget mumbled into her pillow.

'That's right. The boys could manage their bubbles straight away; but when the man popped Alasha inside hers she reached for a hand hole and bruised her knuckles on the edge of it. Then she bumped her head on the roof of the bubble. She tried to walk, lost her balance and fell over. The bubble rolled over on the floor. It was rolling over and over in the white room with Alasha tumbling over and over inside it. Alasha was crying. The man picked her up, bubble and all, pulled her feet through the holes and set her down the right way up. After that she learned to shuffle about, but she still kept hurting herself.'

'Why, Amy? Was she clumsy? Was she stupid?'

'Of course not. How would you feel if you had to live in a bubble? It was the boys who were stupid for not making a fuss.'

'She wasn't good at school though, was she?'

'She could have been if she wanted. It wouldn't have made any difference.'

'Why not?'

'I told you. She was the only girl. No one took any notice of her.'

'She could read,' protested Bridget.

'Of course she could read. She read thousands and thousands of books. She read magazines.'

'Where did the magazines come from, Amy? Why did the men keep them?'

'From the library, silly. They kept them in case they needed them. Anyway she was reading a magazine when she fell in love. That was when she was ten years old.'

'Did you fall in love when you were ten years old?'

'The story's not about me. It's about Alasha and Alasha is ten years old and she is sitting on a window seat with her knees drawn up inside her bubble. Her hands are sticking out of the handholes, turning over the pages of *Woman's Own*. Beside her on the floor is a huge pile of magazines and two sticks with wool twisted round them. Alasha has been teaching herself to knit from a pattern in *Woman's Own*. Now she's bored with knitting. She's alone in the room. It is a small, high-up room and it's very dusty because no one else has been in it for centuries.'

'It's a secret room,' Bridget's words were slurred with sleep. 'Alasha's own room.'

'Sort of. There she sits reading and she looks up from her magazine and out of the window and sees Gidaw and falls in love.'

'How does she know he's called Gidaw? Why does she fall in love with him?'

'She asks people who he is; later on. She falls in love with him because he is tall and because when he turns she sees he has bright green eyes. But he doesn't see her.' Amy stopped. 'Bridget,' she said, 'have you gone to sleep? Don't you want to know who Gidaw was?'

'What's Gidaw?' Max asked next morning. Amy sat facing him across the table in his tiny kitchen, drinking coffee.

'Who, not what. Why?'

'You were talking about Gidaw in your sleep. I wondered what it meant.'

'Actually he was a boy at my junior school. I ran after him.'

'Where to?'

'In sports when we did running. And I invited him to my eleventh birthday party. He was the only boy there.'

'What happened?'

'Nothing. Are you crazy? We were eleven years old.'

'Fair enough.' Max took a sip of coffee. 'What are you working on today?'

'The same: the piece about elderly people on low incomes. What are you doing?'

'Not much. I might go to the launderette.' And a lot of money that would bring in, Amy thought.

She dressed, let herself out of Max's flat and returned to her own place. She made coffee, went into her study, sat in her typing chair and rested her elbows on her desk on either side of the Amstrad keyboard. She looked at the litter of papers on her desk, at the round, brown stains from countless mugs of coffee. She really must tidy up, she thought. She would do it when she finished the article. She switched on the Amstrad, inserted a new disc and began to type.

'Alasha is a woman now,' she typed. 'She works at the bubble factory. She wears white trousers and a white cap and sits in the section where the components for new bubbles are checked – a huge, high-roofed room like a warehouse. In front of her is a conveyor belt which carries rims for handholes and footholes and segments of the transparent stuff of which the bubbles are made. She is supposed to pick them up as they pass and test their strength; but she doesn't. She knits instead, in cable stitch, then in Fair Isle patterns. On each side of her sits a line of men. Behind her a wide drain runs from end to end of the room; liquid flows in it. When a man spots a substandard component he tosses it over his shoulder into the drain and it is carried away to be recycled.

Alasha shows her knitting to the man on her left. He is Gidaw but he does not know she knows that. He asks, "What is it for?"

Amy stopped typing. Bridget always interrupted at that point, she remembered. 'Amy,' Bridget would ask, 'did Alasha choose the seat next to Gidaw on purpose?'

'Of course she did,' Amy would reply. 'On her very first day. Before anyone else could.'

She bent over the keyboard again and typed, 'Alasha pauses. She watches the stream of components pass by and imagines she is watching a real stream; she is watching cool water race over yellow and brown chips of gravel stone. She is watching from a green bank of scratchy, cow-cropped grass. It is hot; there are butterflies and buttercups. And Gidaw says, "It is pretty."'

Amy stopped typing again. What did she think she was doing, she demanded of herself. She had money to earn.

She pressed 'Exit' on the keyboard, changed discs and looked at the notes she had prepared on pensioners. Some of the interview material was dynamite but she couldn't work out how to organise the facts and figures. Nor what to do about Max. She sighed. Perhaps she should narrow it down and write only about elderly women? After all, there were more of them and many of them were much older – and therefore frailer – than the men. And perhaps she shouldn't think about Max.

She thought about Max. She thought about when she first spotted him at a party; he was leaning idly against the mantelpiece on the other side of the room. She thought about how she decided, straight away, that he was the most beautiful man she had ever seen. She thought about how she instantly loved his sleepy green eyes, his thick, red, curly hair. She thought about the way she strode straight across the room and asked him who he was. Amy lapsed into a delicious memory.

After a brief conversation (not a particularly interesting one, so Amy didn't bother to think about that) she suggested they leave the party in search of something to eat. Max agreed. They found an Indian restaurant. While they were eating Max talked and Amy looked at him. Then she listened to him; she loved the sound of his voice but he was talking about fossils. Amy did not know much about fossils, so she changed the subject to food – Indian first, obviously, then Chinese, Japanese and finally Spanish. She hoped they were really discussing whether and when they would make love. They finished eating, split the bill and went to Max's flat where they made love. In the mini cab home afterwards Amy considered how long she should wait before phoning him. At least three days she decided, four if she could manage it.

But the next afternoon Max phoned her. 'Hello,' he said and she imagined him smiling slowly as he spoke, 'are we seeing each other later on, or what?' Of course they were.

They continued to see each other; sometimes they ate out, sometimes they didn't bother to eat; but Amy always went to Max's flat and they always made love there. She cut down her clothes budget to cover the cost of mini cabs home.

She sighed again; she must finish this piece. She forced herself to concentrate on the statistics on her screen. The basic old age pension is £43.60 per week for a single person, she read, and £69.80 for a couple. £10,000 of annuity today buys £1,000 in old age. From the year 2000 benefits will be cut. Somewhere in all these facts was a story. She frowned as she tried to ferret it out.

By 7.30 p.m. she still hadn't. She stopped work, went into the kitchen, looked in the fridge, found a lump of cheese and a loaf from which she cut thick slices and stood eating and worrying at the same time. Then she went to Max's flat. She found the door on the latch and Max sprawled in an armchair, drinking a can of Heineken and playing solitaire. He looked up at her and smiled. 'You still haven't taken my spare key,' he said. 'You're welcome to it any time.'

She ignored his words, sat on the sofa and asked, 'Max, have you been doing that all day?'

'Not all day,' he replied. He looked at his watch. 'Probably about the last couple of hours I should think.'

'Max, tell me, what exactly do you do?'

'Depends on what comes up. Different things. I've only twice ever made this come out right.' He took a peg out of a hole, considered, then replaced it. 'I had it down to two pegs earlier.'

'But what are those different things?'

'I said. This and that. It's all above board. Do you want to have a go?'

'No I don't. Take an average day,' she persisted. 'today, for instance. After I left here, what then?'

He looked uncomfortable. 'I don't ask you what you do all day,' he said.

'But I want to know.'

'I don't see why.'

Amy went to bed early. The sheets were dirty so Max hadn't been to the launderette after all. She was damned if she would wash them tomorrow; she was busy. Later Max joined her, but she rolled away from him. How could she possibly make love when she didn't know what he'd been doing?

He switched off the light and Amy tried to pretend that he wasn't there.

'Once upon a time, far in the future,' she began silently, 'Alasha was sitting at the conveyor in the bubble factory. She told Gidaw. "Last night I had a dream. I dreamt I was swimming in warm water, far out to sea. The water was right up to my neck. I felt very happy although there was no land in sight."'

' "In the dream I could swim," she added, "although when I go to the swimming pool I can't."

'The man on her right said abruptly, "Dreams are not allowed. Dreams are mad. Dreams aren't true."

'Alasha sat up straight. "Knit two, slip one, knit two, pass slip stitch over," she said under her breath.

'"It could come true," said Gidaw who was sitting on her left, "she could learn how to swim."

'Next day she announced, "Last night I dreamt I had to go somewhere important. There were only two routes. I could walk across a tightrope through blue, sunshiny air. I knew I would fall off the tightrope. Or I could squeeze through a small tunnel. Its black walls contracted; it became narrower and narrower."

'"You don't have anywhere important to go," said the man on her right. "Otherwise you wouldn't be here."

'"Which did you choose?" asked Gidaw.

'"I woke up while I was forcing myself into the tunnel, trying to push the walls of the tunnel apart. It wasn't very nice."

'"Will you tell me your dream tomorrow?" he asked, but the next day war was declared and they were too busy talking about that to discuss dreams.'

'What was the war about, Amy?' asked Bridget. 'Who was fighting?'

'I don't know,' Amy replied. 'The story's about Alasha, not about the war. I can only tell you what happened to her. And I'm tired. That's all for tonight.'

'You were dreaming again,' said Max in the morning, over coffee. 'You shouted something. I couldn't catch what.'

'So?' said Amy. She looked at him. His red hair was rumpled and he was wearing an old sweatshirt and jeans. How could he hold down any sort of job when he looked like that? 'So,' she repeated, 'are you playing solitaire again today?'

'The weather's too nice.' He gazed dreamily out of the window. 'I could take photographs I think,' he said, 'if the light stays like this.' Amy rose sharply to her feet and demanded, 'Don't you ever do anything useful?' The pain in Max's green eyes made it essential that she say something worse. 'I bet you've never had a proper job in your life,' she stormed. 'You probably don't even pay your National Insurance contributions,' she accused. 'You wait till you're a pensioner,' she threatened. He didn't answer. 'Some of us have to work for a living,' she shouted into the silence, then slammed out of his flat and went home.

For a while she paced around her living room. She said, 'Calm down. He isn't worth it,' several times out loud while she walked. Eventually she stopped. Today was positively the last day for finishing the piece about pensioners. She went into her study, switched on the Amstrad and inserted a disc.

'With the outbreak of war,' she typed carefully, 'the demand for bubbles increased because so many were damaged in the fighting. As fast as the factory workers checked the components for new bubbles, the drain behind them was choked with bits of bubbles that were broken in battle; some had scraps of flesh clinging to them; the drain began to smell nasty.

'The conveyor belt was adjusted to a higher speed; up-beat music played over the tannoy. The supervisor even tried to make Alasha work; but gave up when he realised she could not be relied upon to detect a fault which might cost a life.

'"Why can't you concentrate?" complained the man on her right.

'"I never have. Besides I am knitting."

'"Our work is important now. The bubbles save lives."

'"If we weren't protected by the bubbles in the first place, maybe we wouldn't want to fight."

'Next day their bubbles were taken away because every last one was needed for the war effort. Alasha had a new idea. "Let's pretend to be mirrors," she suggested to Gidaw. "I'll tell you how you look. Then you tell me."

'"You have dark hairs on the backs of your fingers," she began.

'"I know that," he replied. "I can see them."

'"Your nose is big and bumpy," she tried next.

'He raised a hand to it, "I know. I can feel it."

'"Your hair is brown."

'"I know. I've seen it."

'"When?" his hair was too short for him to see it.

'"When it is cut. The pieces that fall on the floor."

'"You can't see your eyes. They're green. Now me."

'"You have a pale face," he said slowly. 'Your nose is small. Your eyes are black. I can't see your hair. What colour is it?" She drew a tress from the band of her cap and showed him. "Black," she said, then told him her latest dream. "Last night you were in the tunnel with me," she said, "I was the one who pushed the walls apart. They were black and shiny."

'At regular intervals the music was interrupted by announcements of victories. When this happened Alasha spoke more loudly than usual and Gidaw often missed a whole batch of components as he listened to what she said.'

Amy stopped, went into her kitchen, made a cup of coffee and worried briefly and intensely about the article she wasn't writing. It was all Max's fault, she thought crossly. Everything was fine, everything was wonderful right up until three evenings ago. As usual they were at Max's flat. As usual they made love in Max's bed. As usual Amy switched on the light and checked her watch. It was even later than usual. She yawned and complained, 'I wish I hadn't so far to go home,' and Max replied, 'You could always stay.'

Amy was comfortable, sleepy and warm. For once she couldn't face the thought of dressing and phoning a cab and of the cold journey home. She said carefully, 'Yes, I suppose I could. If I get up very, very early tomorrow.'

Max went on, 'You could stay any time you want. I'll lend you my spare key so you can have one cut for yourself.' She stayed.

Next morning Amy rose at seven, slipped out of bed, dressed and sat in Max's living room wondering what it would feel like to be old and poor. She continued wondering until it was time for the shops to open so she could visit a locksmith, then realised that Max had fallen asleep without giving her the key. She opened the bedroom door; Max was still asleep. She let herself out and returned to her own flat where she went into the study, switched on the Amstrad and wondered – where would she work when she moved in with Max?

Of course, she didn't have to sell her flat, she reasoned; but she wouldn't be able to contribute to his mortgage while she still had one of her own. Or should she suggest she use some of the capital realised from the sale of her property to reduce the mortgage on his? In which case they would need to transfer ownership of his place into both their names.

What about day-to-day expenses? Would they each put in a certain amount each week and would that be fair, given she ate less than Max? Would they split gas and electricity bills; water rates; tv/video rental; building insurance; contents insurance; ground rent? Max's flat was in a mansion block so maybe he was liable for a service charge for which she would have to budget.

Then there was the phone. She used it so frequently she should perhaps pay more than half of Max's bill. She must ask him if he rented the receiver from British Telecom or if he had bought it, which was more economical in the long run.

She looked round her study, at the messy desk, at the overfull bookcases and the heaps of files. There were files in the bedroom too and more books in the lounge, not to mention her clothes and furniture and cooking things. Would there be room for all this stuff in his place or would she have to put some of it in store? How much would that cost per month? Even if she threw some of it away she would still have to hire a van to take it to the dump. On the other hand, she would save on cabs. And she could rent a market stall and sell some things – what would she have to pay for a day's rent in Camden Lock, say? She took her pocket calculator out of the drawer, then put it back. She must work; she needed money.

But Amy didn't write her article. Instead she stood in her kitchen and gazed out of the window. She tasted her coffee; it was lukewarm. Never mind. She carried it into the study and put the mug on the desk beside the keyboard.

'Several times a day,' she typed, 'there were the chants. Led by a voice from the tannoy the workers would repeat the names of the victories, shouting in unison and stamping their feet between each chant. Alasha did not shout. Gidaw tried, but kept shouting the wrong name. He took to waiting until each word began, to give him an idea of what it might be, before he dared join in. But still he was often wrong. He fell silent.

'At night Alasha slept in her secret room, high above the ground. She woke from her dreams to horror: dull, distant thuds, screaming sirens, the sound of something huge crashing to the ground. She rose, peered out of the window and saw gold and red flames leaping against the black sky, saw the black shape of a missile descend on a nearby dormitory, saw people, limp like rag dolls, propelled into the crimson sky by the force of the explosion. She returned to bed and curled up, pressing a knuckle against her mouth.

'In the morning there were gaps on either side of the conveyor belt. The music played faster, the tea break was shorter and the voice on the tannoy exhorted everyone to chant more loudly. Towards noon, injured workers began to straggle in. Some had blood on their clothes, others wore stained bandages. They settled in their places beside the conveyor belt, began work and joined, rather raggedly, in the chants. "Come on, workers," shouted the voice on the tannoy, "I want to hear you chant." Mid-chant there was a tremendous crash. The lights went out; Alasha heard screams of pain; the tannoy continued to bellow, "One. Two. Three." The smell from the drain became overpowering; she felt liquid from it flow over her feet. She stuffed her knitting in the front of her shirt and reached for Gidaw's wrist. "We must go," she told him and pulled him after her.

'She groped in the darkness for the edge of the drain and followed it, wading through foul, swirling water. The voice on the tannoy gurgled and stopped. The screams of pain continued. Alasha bumped against warm, writhing bodies and struggled on, still gripping Gidaw, until they reached the end of the drain and stumbled out into grey, afternoon light. She pulled Gidaw across the road between high buildings; Alasha turned as she ran, saw the factory explode in flames and ran faster – through the industrial estate and into a street of shops. The shops were still brightly-lit; plaster mannequins wearing scarlet and cloth-of-gold posed in the windows.

'A crash. A window shattered. The dummies fell apart. The scarlet and gold cloth was torn to shreds. In the sky above Alasha and Gidaw an aircraft veered, crumpled and crashed into the city's buildings. Alasha pulled Gidaw along streets and down alleyways, glancing from side to side for signs of danger. They came to a deserted, main road; telephone wires trailed across the cracked tarmac; an armoured car stood by the kerb; two men in khaki uniform lay half in, half out of it. "Quick," said Alasha. She ran to the vehicle. "The driver's legs are tangled in the controls. Help me pull him out." Gidaw pulled; he was strong and moved the corpse easily. Alasha jumped into the driving seat; Gidaw swung up beside her and they were off.

'Hours later they reached the edge of the city. Silence. The darkness of the countryside. They passed a church on their left. On the hillside ahead Alasha saw the lights of a village. She came to a pair of gates, stopped the car, climbed down and opened the gates, drove through and climbed down again to close them. She followed a narrow driveway until she came to a low, rambling house. Light gleamed from a single window. She stopped the car, turned off the engine and rescued her knitting from inside her shirt. She counted her stitches. She hadn't dropped one.

'She turned to Gidaw. "We will be safe here," she told him. "I will dream of better things," and kissed him.'

Amy stopped typing. That was the end of the story. When she reached that point she went to sleep and started again at the beginning the next night. Bridget was always furious; but it was understandable that an eleven-year-old couldn't imagine what happened next. She ought to be able to do so now.

She thought for a moment. Simple. They would live happily ever after, of course. The war would end. Gidaw would find a job and earn good money – there would be a massive demand for strong, young men to rebuild the city. Because Alasha was of child-bearing age (the means of reproducing without women was destroyed in the war) they would be eligible for subsidised housing. Alasha would bring in a bit extra by teaching knitting two evenings a week at the local Adult Education Institute. Soon they would be able to afford a mortgage on a starter home or to take advantage of their right to buy the flat they rented. Alasha would handle the family finances; each week she would take Gidaw's wages and set aside carefully-calculated sums for housekeeping, clothes, shoes, holidays, household repairs, home improvements, life insurance and personal pension plans.

Alasha would know everything Gidaw did and what it cost. She would know – to the penny – how much he spent in the pub each evening, she would know – to the minute – how long he spent in the loo each morning and how much loo paper he used – would know all the boring, intimate, details of his daily life which, Amy realised with a rush of relief, she had absolutely no interest in learning about Max.

She changed discs and plunged straight into her article. She put aside the facts; she would go for the personal approach. She transcribed three of her interviews with elderly women; their own voices would say more about their plight than any amount of figures could. She worked on, oblivious of the time. When she finally paused and looked at her watch she found it was gone nine. She read through the piece. It was good. She took out her pocket calculator and did a sum. The fee would comfortably cover – at least a month's supply of mini cabs.

THE SECTION HEAD

The Section Head hung his dark blue raincoat on the hook reserved for him. Carrie said into the telephone, 'Accommodation Section. Can I help you?' her voice rising on the penultimate syllable of each sentence as Mrs Butteridge had taught her.

The Section Head sat at his desk. He shook snow over the skiers in his paperweight as he always did first thing in the morning and said 'Mrs Butteridge. My diary,' as he always did, second thing.

But he had no opportunity to pursue his routine further. 'Dave,' said Bob, bending anxiously over the Section Head's desk. 'Dave,' Bob repeated, 'it's Wendover Buildings again, Dave. Proposals for complete refurbishment. And all the staff to be relocated before the contractors start work.'

Accommodation Section was responsible for moving people: people who were employed by the Corporation, that is. Accommodation Section did not do the actual moving. The staff of the Section did not pack other people's books into cartons or heave around filing cabinets or drive the trucks that transported office furniture to new locations; the staff of Accommodation Section were all on executive, not manual, grades.

What the staff of the Section did was to plan the moves according to the overall requirements of the Corporation. Then they notified the departments concerned, arranged for transport and requisitioned new telephone systems.

Accommodation Section itself had moved twelve times in the last eighteen months. Once this was to make more space for itself, once it was to make more space for Forward Development. When the Corporation expanded the Section moved to Headquarters; when there were cuts it moved to a tiny cubby-hole of an office.

For some weeks now there had been a period of stability. All the same, the people who worked in Accommodation Section were not always sure where they worked. Some of them found themselves arriving at the wrong Tube station in the morning. Others found themselves walking in the wrong direction when they came out of the right station. David Reynolds, the Section Head, was lenient whenever someone turned up late saying, 'I forgot we weren't still at Blakeney Mansions.' Though he sometimes suspected that Carrie had simply overslept.

David Reynolds was unsure himself whether the Section would stay in its current location long enough to make it worthwhile unpacking all his personal possessions. He had unearthed his blotter, pens, paper and paper clips because they were in daily use: also the little paperweight containing a snowscene with two skiers. But the silver-framed photo of Lou with Patrick and Elizabeth was somewhere in one of the boxes. So were many other items essential to the team's efficiency. Others, though unpacked, never found a permanent home. That would be a waste of effort when the Section might have to up sticks again soon; but it did mean the office was rather a mess.

When David Reynolds had arrived that morning he had been pleased to find Carrie already at her desk. As usual she had been doing several things at once. She was holding the telephone receiver clamped between shoulder and ear. She was chewing. With one hand she fiddled with a crusty bread roll, slightly dented and oozing brown from the first couple of bites, on a paper bag on her desk. With the other she tapped a few words onto the typewriter in front of her. 'Sausage and pickle,' she said out of the corner of her mouth into the phone. 'What have you got? Did you really?' she asked. 'I thought you didn't like coleslaw.' She raised the roll towards her mouth, then put it down again. 'Hang on. Won't be a tic.' She looked up and said, 'Good morning, Mr Reynolds.'

The staff of Accommodation Section all worked for David Reynolds, but they did not all address him in the same way; he insisted on that. To Carrie, Angela and Tony the messenger, David Reynolds was Mr Reynolds. To Mrs Butteridge he was David Reynolds. Only to Bob, the Deputy Section Head of Accommodation Section, was he Dave.

'Well,' said the Section Head to Bob. 'Have you found the old specifications for Wendover Buildings?'

'Mrs Butteridge discovered them behind the chest with the plans in it. You have to advise the Management Board. At eleven this morning.'

'Just like that?' Bob nodded. David Reynolds shook his head. 'It isn't on. They must give more notice if they expect serious comments.'

'It seems they did. We didn't see the memo.'

David Reynolds knew what that meant. Someone had lost it. Probably Carrie or Tony. Angela never lost anything. Mrs Butteridge only found things. And if such a memo ever reached Bob he would hand it to Dave straight away to offload the responsibility.

'I'll deal with that later,' said the Section Head. 'What about those specifications?'

Bob was not able to give the full picture. Some of his notes from the telephone conversation with the Secretary to the Management Board were legible. Some were not. He must have been panicking.

David Reynolds did not attend Board meetings as a rule. He preferred to keep his head down. Being on the spot could so easily draw attention. He was, nonetheless, the Section Head and would do his duty by his team. The team did their duty by him too. When the phone rang Carrie said firmly, 'I'm afraid Mr Reynolds is unavailable at the moment,' and then, eagerly, 'Can I help at all?' Bob returned to his desk to have a shot at putting the instructions from the Secretary to the Management Board down on paper. Angela assembled the old specifications for Wendover Buildings in the correct order. Mrs Butteridge wrote 'Wendover Buildings' in round script on a brown folder. Tony collected the plans from Angela and the folder from Mrs Butteridge. He carried them to Bob. Bob checked the work of his juniors. He added his own notes to the folder. Tony carried the folder to the Section Head.

David Reynolds arrived at the Board Room several minutes early. The Room always depressed him. Perhaps it was the dark, panelled walls; perhaps it was the gilt-framed portraits of the former Partners in the Corporation or the huge, highly-polished rectangular table. He selected one of the green, leather-upholstered chairs, settled his slim file of papers on the table in front of it and exchanged news with a couple of other middle managers.

On the dot of eleven the Chief Executive entered the room. He was followed by a woman David Reynolds had not seen before: a new secretary perhaps?

The Chief Executive sat down. He cleared his throat. 'Miss Winters. . .' he began.

'Ms,' said the woman who was now sitting beside him. She looked around cheerfully, as though she were welcome.

The Chief Executive rearranged his papers on the table.

'Ms Winters,' he announced to the meeting. 'Our new Director of Manpower and Resources. As you know the appointment was made in person by the Partners, in conjunction with officials from the Equal Opportunities and Business Enterprise bodies. I am sure I do not need to remind you all that the Corporation, by being seen to have taken such an initiative, places itself in a most advantageous position in respect of this year's Management for Excellence Awards.'

David Reynolds had not known. He had been keeping his head down.

'The post,' the Chief Executive continued, 'is in overall command of four sections. Ms Winters, allow me to introduce you to your section heads.' He picked them out one by one, 'Personnel, O & M, Central Services and Accommodation.' David Reynolds nodded like the others.

'Ms Winters,' the Chief Executive went on. 'May I welcome you on all our behalves to the Corporation and to the Management Board. Perhaps you wish to say a few words?'

'Thank you,' said the woman. 'First, I propose my title be changed to "Director of Employees and Resources". The total workforce of the Corporation is over eight thousand, right? And at least half of the employees are women.'

For a moment no one spoke. Then, 'If you could perhaps clarify your point?' said the Chief Executive.

'Manpower,' said the woman. 'Manpower excludes womanpower.'

Her proposal was agreed unanimously. No one wished to be seen to jeopardise the Corporation's chance of receiving the Management for Excellence Award.

She started talking again. David Reynolds inspected her. She was wearing a neat blue blouse. That was fine. But her hair was far too wild. The way it sprung up and away from her brow and tumbled down her back! It was red but there was something odd about it, darker streaks. She must dye it he decided, then realised that the Chief Executive was talking to him.

'Section Head of Accommodation Section,' the Chief Executive was saying. 'Could you give the Board your views on these proposals?'

David Reynolds looked the Chief Executive in the eye. 'Under the circumstances. . . The question undoubtedly requires further in-depth analysis. . . I shall put one of my people on it as a matter of urgency.'

'Why?' asked Ms Winters.

'I think, Director, once you know the Corporation a little better. . .'

'I'd like to. Tell me, what would the people in your section think?'

'Think?' said the Section Head. 'I speak for the section.'

'Everyone has a voice of their own.' She smiled. 'I'll want to hear from them all. After all, they could be facing major changes in their working practices. Let's say Tuesday at your office. Ten-thirty. We'd better set aside the whole day.'

Back at his own desk David Reynolds could not rid himself of a feeling of unease. He fixed his mind, with an effort, on the first task in hand. He rapped his desk with his paperweight. Snow flurried in the air around the skiers. 'Bob. A word please,' he said. 'Then I shall want to speak to you, Mrs Butteridge, then Carrie, Angela and Tony. In that order.'

He interrogated them one after the other about the missing memo, without success. He sat back to consider the more serious issue. should he call a staff meeting and tell them about the new Director's intention to visit them and ask them what they thought? No doubt that's exactly what Ms Womanpower would do in the same circumstances. He shook his head sharply. Or did he, through his superior knowledge of the Corporation, hold a trump card?

'Mrs Butteridge,' he said. 'The register, please.'

Accommodation Section kept the Corporation's register of premises. The register contained details of square metreage, rateable value, market rent, structural condition, existing facilities, previous occupiers, date to be brought into use, if not currently in use, and future recommended use of every single building the Corporation owned. There was only the one copy of the register.

It was the work of a few moments to find what he wanted. He placed his ruler below the entry on the relevant page, highlighted the entry and said, 'Bob. A staff meeting immediately. Inform the section.'

Bob, Mrs Butteridge, Carrie, Angela and Tony dragged their chairs towards his desk.

David Reynolds rapped his paperweight. He waited for the snow to settle on the shoulders of the skiers. 'The Section,' he announced, 'is to move. To Allstrop House.'

'The move is to be completed by close of play Monday,' he went on. 'Today is Wednesday, so time is short. We will begin this afternoon.'

It was a tradition in Accommodation Section that each member of staff packed his or her own belongings, although the heavy work of moving was, of course, left to blue-collar operatives from the Labour Department. The staff of Accommodation Section set to work.

All went well at Allstrop House the first week after they moved. They settled in, so far as they ever settled in anywhere. Bob had yet another word with Carrie and her typing began to improve. David Reynolds taught Angela the principles of writing a memo. Mrs Butteridge, diligent as ever, found, in a forgotten cardboard carton, the long-lost specification for Lindmere Mews, an attractive period property which the Corporation had acquired as part of a bad debt. Every morning Tony the messenger waited at Accommodation Section's previous office, their official location, to collect the mail. The Section Head wrote reports, made comments on other people's reports and dispatched them via Tony to Headquarters. In short, thought the Section Head, they made a good team.

More important, nobody found the Section, although somebody must have been looking.

Then, the second Monday morning, no Carrie. David Reynolds didn't worry. At the beginning of the week Carrie often had a problem remembering where she worked. At eleven-thirty, when she still had not arrived, he instructed Mrs Butteridge to telephone Carrie's home number. As the files were even more disorganised than usual after the last hasty move, it was twelve o'clock before she was able to find the number. David Reynolds decided to take both Angela and her off whatever else Bob had given them to do and put them onto filing, top priority.

Carrie was not at home, Mrs Butteridge reported. Her mother was sure she had gone into work, but could not confirm to which office. 'She moves about a lot,' said Carrie's mother. 'She says it goes with the job.'

David Reynolds dispatched Tony to Accommodation Section's last office to see if Carrie was there.

He straightened thirty-four paper clips. With the end of one he poked dirt from under a finger nail. He shook snow over the skiers several times. Angela gave him a draft memo and he replaced 'Thank you for writing to me yesterday,' with 'I refer to your memorandum of the sixteenth'.

One p.m. Tony returned without news of Carrie. David Reynolds told him he must go without a lunch hour; there were urgent packages to deliver. David Reynolds lunched at a sandwich bar.

Two-thirty. Still no sign of Carrie. David Reynolds told Angela to look after the switchboard which she hated. He told Mrs Butteridge to make tea for the entire office which was not her job. He straightened more paper clips. The afternoon wore on.

It was after four-thirty when Carrie finally turned up. 'What is the explanation of this?' demanded the Section Head.

'I overslept. Then I went to the old office by mistake. Then I met Deborah. I had lunch with her. She's coming to see you.'

'Deborah?'

'Ms Winters. Our new boss. She's great. Not like a boss at all. I've been telling her all about what we do here. Ten-thirty tomorrow morning she's coming.'

The Section Head instructed everyone to be at his or her desk by nine sharp the next morning; and for once everyone was. By ten-fifteen the floor was clear, no crates or cardboard boxes. The desks were tidy. The plans were all in the plan chest, the files all filed, though many in the wrong drawers.

The Section Head rang Forward Development and Central Services and arranged for them to make regular phone calls to Accommodation Section during the course of the morning. Then he gave each of his members of staff a suitable task with which to be occupied.

'Place is like a bloody army camp,' David Reynolds heard Tony, who was stuffing an enormous pile of envelopes, mutter to Carrie.

It was not, thought the Section Head as he cast his eye over his people, an accurate remark. Carrie had clearly made an effort. She had pulled her hair out of her eyes and for once she was not wearing a teeshirt with a picture on it, though her blouse had parted company with her skirt. Angela, he noted with approval, looked as neat as ever, in a dark outfit with a white collar. But she also looked sulky for which there was no justification as he had given her the perfectly straightforward task of drafting a requisition to Supplies Department for a consignment of paper clips.

Mrs Butteridge, grey-haired, plump, dependable, sat stiffly at her desk compiling a list of those of the Corporation's premises that had access to a fax machine. A frown creased her forehead as her forefinger moved slowly down a page of the register. Mrs Butteridge was the backbone of the office, he had to give her that. But no dynamism about her, no get-up-and-go.

Bob was wearing a suit, white shirt and dark, striped tie. Entirely appropriate for the Deputy Section Head. Unfortunately, the knot of his tie had loosened during the last hour, his collar curled at the edges and there was a red biro mark on the front of his shirt.

Tony was wearing jeans, which the Section Head had expressly told him not to do. On the other hand, now he that he had applied himself to the task, he was filling envelopes with commendable speed. A pity he was jigging rhythmically to some imaginary pop song.

The door of the office opened. 'At last I get to meet you all.' Ms Winters smiled at them. 'I hadn't realised you'd moved. People do seem to move a lot in the Corporation.'

The Section Head rose from his desk and extended his hand. 'We pride ourselves on our swift response to the changing needs of the Corporation.'

'So how do you want to play it, David?' she asked.

'I assume you and I will discuss things.'

'To be honest, I prefer a collective approach.'

David Reynolds sighed. He summoned the others to his desk. He said, 'Ms Winters, the new Director of Employees and Resources.' He introduced them to her, adding to each name a brief job description.

'Thank you for that, David,' said Ms Winters. 'Now I'd like each of you to tell me about your job in your own words.'

Mrs Butteridge looked anxious. Angela blushed. Bob clasped his hands. Tony gazed at the woman in a most inappropriate way. Carrie did nothing, even when the phone rang.

'Why don't we switch on the answerphone?' suggested Ms Winters. Carrie did so. 'That's better. Now we can have our discussion in peace.'

Each of the staff then repeated his or her job description as accurately as possible. Tony, the last, only managed, 'I carry things around. When Mr Reynolds says.'

'Let's try it another way.' Ms Winters smiled again. 'What do you think is important about what you do? What's its value to the Corporation?'

'Dunno,' said Tony. 'Nothing really.'

'All right. Can you tell me what you like about your work?' The Section Head shook an avalanche onto the heads of the skiers. Tony was paid to do his job, not to like it.

'I quite like walking. And driving. Getting out and about. I time myself to see how quickly I can get places.'

'Don't you think that's valuable to the Corporation?'

'Not especially. Sometimes I time myself to see how slowly I can get somewhere. You know, without actually stopping.'

The Section Head coughed. 'This is a disciplinary matter, Director,' he said.

'Doesn't worry me,' said Tony. 'I can always get another job.'

'It's simpler if you all call me Deborah,' Ms Winters went on. 'Tony, how do you think your job could be made more interesting?'

'Dunno. Not like it is anyway. I mean it's crazy having a messenger for each section. If there was a central pool of messengers you could have a proper rota though. Save yourselves a bit of time that way. Not that it matters.'

'Interesting idea. And not one I've heard before. We'll see if it's feasible. Thank you, Tony.'

'Mrs Butteridge,' Ms Winters continued. 'What would you say you do best?' Mrs Butteridge looked at the Section Head. Carrie looked at Ms Winters. 'She finds things,' said Carrie.

'Why do they get lost?'

'It's my fault.' Everyone looked at Carrie. 'I told you yesterday Deborah. I get lost as well as losing things. I'm the worst but everyone does it a bit. Except Mrs Butteridge.'

The Section Head realised that he was still clasping his paperweight. Looking down at his hand, he saw that one of the skiers had broken away from its base and now lay prone, like a corpse, in the snow. He put the paperweight down. The snow settled.

'I'm untidy. I eat at my desk sometimes,' Carrie went on in a rush. 'When I get lost or lose things I make up excuses sometimes. And I chat. Bob says so. People phone up and I don't just deal with the query and put the phone down. I chat to them. I know I shouldn't. Bob gets in a panic about it. In case someone important's trying to get through. But I like chatting.'

Angela said suddenly, 'I don't want to learn to write memos.' Bob said, 'It's not that I panic often. It's just when there's a crisis.'

'What would you prefer to do, Angela?' asked Ms Winters. 'I'll come to you next, Bob.'

They soon became so deeply involved they decided, on a vote, not to stop for lunch. Tony and Ms Winters went out together with a bulk order for sandwiches. Bob and Mrs Butteridge made tea or coffee for all of them. Carrie and Angela, without being asked, dealt with all the telephone messages, most of which were fictitious requests for information from Forward Development or Central Services.

Somewhere around four o'clock the Section Head became aware that the meeting was drawing to a close.

It appeared they all still had plenty to say. Between them they had come up with proposals for the reorganisation of the section and for changes in its relationship with a number of other sections, improvements in record-keeping, a system for monitoring their own efficiency and now they were keen to get on with the work. They would have a preliminary outline completed by the end of the week.

The woman rose to leave amid a babble of voices. The Section Head followed her. 'Director,' he said.

'Do call me Deborah.'

'Yes, of course. Absolutely. A word in private if I may.'

In the corridor David Reynolds played for time. 'I just wanted to express, as Section Head, how much I appreciate the personal interest you have shown in my staff. It is, may I say, most refreshing to have a Director who is so concerned about the welfare of the personnel. I am sure they will work all the better for it.'

He returned to the office. 'One moment,' he said to his staff. 'I have spoken to the Director. We have important work ahead of us. However, before we begin I have to tell you all that it has been decided that the Section is to move. The notice is, I am afraid, very short. We are to vacate these premises by tomorrow night.'

On Thursday at nine-thirty the Section Head arrived at the new office on the second floor of Lindmere Mews. He had thought that Carrie might turn up late. But there was no sign of anyone belonging to the section, although some of the cartons had been delivered. They couldn't all be lost. They could, perhaps, be late. It was a longer walk to here from the Tube.

The Section Head sat down at a desk by the window. Below was a small square surrounded by wrought iron railings: grass in the centre, some shrubs, a bed of pink roses, a couple of trees. He watched a road sweeper with a cart come round the corner into the square. At the further end of the square he could see something red and white in the gutter: a coca cola can, a crumpled carrier or even a small rag? He watched the sweeper approach it. The sweeper moved on, head bent, but the object remained. No pride in his work, though the Section Head.

He turned away from the window and unpacked a few essentials; he arranged his leather-bound blotter, paper clips, the paperweight with the skiers, a biro and his fountain pen on his desk. He found the file with the list of home numbers but did not call any of them.

At twelve-thirty on the dot he set off for lunch. He discovered a pleasant Italian restaurant just around the corner. He ordered half a bottle of wine with his meal.

Later in the empty office the Section Head recorded Accommodation Section's new location in the register of premises and deleted the old one. He turned the pages, looking back over lists of buildings. Purpose-built blocks, converted shopfronts, workshops, prime commercial premises, even a few units of tied housing – how many hundreds of times had he moved people in and out of them? How many times and to how many premises had his own section moved over the years? When Ms Womanpower sent for him he would tell her of all that dedicated work.

The wine had been unwise. He dozed a little. Waking with a jerk of his head at a quarter past four, he looked down again at the register. Fishburne Place! Why hadn't he thought of it before? He could make the move on the instant, overnight, as he had only the register and his personal possessions to transport. And where after that? He bent over the register, planning an exacting programme of solitary moves.

Outside, unseen by the Section Head, the road sweeper returned on his way to the Council depot and spotted the coca cola can. 'Filthy habits,' he grumbled. 'Chuck stuff anywhere, some people will.' He picked up the can, placed it in his barrow and trundled away.

In the following months several people caught sight of the Section Head, register under his arm, head down, scurrying through the doorway of one or another of the Corporation's premises. Occasionally he stopped a passing messenger and asked for news. Not that any of the messengers could delay for long now. They worked on a rota; and Tony, their timekeeper, ran a tight ship.

Bit by bit the Section Head pieced together what had happened to the rest of the team. Angela had been transferred to Customer Complaints because she wrote such good, plain English. And the customers stopped complaining – that is, they only complained once instead of penning letter after letter in a fury of frustration at the incomprehensible bureaucratic responses they received.

Carrie went to Public Relations. The press officers rushed about the place, ash from their cigarettes and crumbs from their mid-morning buns dropping in their wake, in a panic over the launch of the second phase of the Management Modernisation Plan. One of them gave Carrie a press release to type; another told Carrie to look after the switchboard. Carrie, phone clamped between left ear and shoulder, chatted in the friendliest of fashions to one caller after another while she typed the press release.

Bob was thrown in at the deep end on his first day too, in Staff Welfare. 'You'll just have to see people and do the best you can,' he was told. 'The first client's due at ten-fifteen.'

Bob rose from his desk as the door opened. A nervous-looking man walked in. Bob moved towards him. Bob tripped on the telephone wire. He saved himself by grasping the edge of the desk. He put out a trembling hand to shake hands. 'I'm afraid I'm new here,' he mumbled. 'I'm afraid I'm not qualified. I won't be any help. Um. . .

I mean. . . But if there was anything I could do. Anything.'
He subsided into silence and chewed his nails.

The man took a deep breath. He heaved a long sigh. He
slumped into a chair. 'You know what it's like, don't you?'
he said. 'You understand. You've no idea what a relief it
is. . . If it were anybody else. . . . But I know I can talk to
you.' Bob was a hit in Staff Welfare.

And what of Mrs Butteridge? She was put in charge of
Lost Property. And she found the Section Head.

Mrs Butteridge could have explained what continued
to puzzle the Section Head, and made him think that
Ms Womanpower hadn't finished with him yet – his salary
was still paid, every month, into his bank account.

Mrs Butteridge could have explained that the Section
Head of Accommodation Section still held the only copy
of the Corporation's register of premises. Without access
to the register no one throughout the whole of the
Corporation was able to move. As a result there was a
fifty per cent increase in efficiency and a thirty per cent
reduction in absenteeism. The Partners included these
achievements in their submission for the Management
for Excellence Award and received the highest commen-
dation. The Partners recorded their appreciation in writing in a memo to the Management Board. The Board
formally agreed that the Section Head was worth his
weight in gold, although it added a rider that it was
only because of the quite exceptional inter-personal skills
of the Director of Employees and Resources which had
brought his hitherto latent talents into play. The Director
of Employees and Resources, as a good manager, tried
to pass on credit where credit was due, but by the time
she visited the office where Mrs Butteridge had found the
Section Head he had gone again.

THE DESTINATION

She had thought a day trip to the country an odd
alternative to the more usual invitation, on a second
meeting with a man, to dinner or to the theatre and to
drinks afterwards. But she had to admit that she liked it
here. The sun was hot and the plants, even the grasses,
high and lush. There were surprises all the time – small
creatures rustling, birds exploding from the trees and a
new enticing view from each corner and hilltop. She found
the walking itself tiring, though not actually unpleasant,
and the little pub where they stopped for lunch was a
delight.

On the man's advice she drank real ale, two half pints
only, given there was a full afternoon's walking ahead. It
was the right thing to drink but it did make her drowsy
and, combined with the noisy doings of insects, birds and
sheep, sexy.

Later, in a piece of wasteland between farms, rosebay
willowherb jostled with the tall, crackling grass. There
was no one about; and it was a beautiful penis the man
had. One hand could circle its column neatly or two
could fan out further down. Penises, she thought, are
so appealing, the best of them. A pity men walk about
all day concealing them in their trousers. With men you

can't tell until they take their clothes off whether it's going to be beautiful or pale, insipid or spectacular.

What does a penis tell you about a man? She tried to frame a question along these lines to ask him. Out of cowardice she said instead, 'I'm a bit uncomfortable like that.'

He was probably offended. Anyway they replaced some clothes, adjusted others and resumed their walk.

The man folded the Ordnance Survey map to a manageable size and explained how its signs and symbols should be read. If she paid attention to the map, she learned, the countryside would not be surprising at all. In London the $A - Z$ took her to her destination but gave no clue as to whether she was headed for a slum or for a terrace of elegant Georgian homes. Not so this map.

'The hill will grow steeper soon,' he predicted. 'Once we're over the brow we'll have a glimpse of a rather large house on the opposite slope at the end of a private road. In the distance, on our right, will be a water tower. On our left will be a non-coniferous copse. After a few yards we will reach a break in the trees and a footpath leading between them. That's where we're going.'

'Surely', she said, 'the map can't really tell us what it's like here.'

'Oh, yes, it can.' He stopped and pointed. 'Look at that small pond we've just passed – here it is on the map. I knew about its marshy perimeter from these symbols. See these countour lines? They tell us we are climbing a hill and they show us how steep it is by how close together they are. And those orchards. There they are, look, quite clearly marked, with the trees in rows.'

'What are we doing it for then? If you know what's coming next?'

'Why do people climb Everest?'

After the break in the trees they progressed from bright sun into the delicious, odorous gloom of a wood. Apart from the ferns, everything was dark and rather squishy. She wanted to stop and bend close to the ground, to peer at any creatures that lived in the leaf mould. The creatures were not on the map of course.

'Don't you think that the map is only a sort of outline?' she asked. 'Like when you plan a holiday, and you study all the brochures and look at pictures of the hotel and the swimming pool and read the guide books, and it's always different when you get there.'

'You should complain to the tour operator,' said the man. 'Or ABTA. That's what they're for.'

'I wouldn't take any notice if I were you,' said a voice which was not the man's.

She shook her head and continued the rhythm of placing one foot, then the other, solidly on the damp brown path.

'I said I wouldn't take any notice,' the voice repeated. 'I'm the boss here.'

She looked sideways to see if he had heard anything but, no, his expression had not changed. He was explaining that they would soon be in open fields and after that they could expect a walk down a narrow lane where a church with a tower, not spire, would be visible to the left.

'I'm the boss,' the voice insisted. It was coming from the crotch of his jeans. 'I know where we're going. He doesn't.'

She giggled and the man asked, 'Why are you laughing?'

'I'm happy to be out in the sun again.'

'What do you think I feel like, then,' said the man's penis, 'trapped in somebody's trousers? Why aren't I allowed out? Am I that ugly?'

'Quite the opposite.'

'What?' said the man, but didn't wait for an answer. 'Could you stop here for a minute? I'm going back into the woods for a pee.'

'No hurry. Take your time.'

He rejoined her and they walked across the wide fields, and the penis, after a short period of silence, started to mutter again, complaining.

'Shut up,' she wanted to say. 'No, we can't stop and let you take a peek. We're here to follow the route, cover the miles, confirm what's on the map, not to indulge you. Anyway you should be used to it. You've been in trousers for years.'

'What makes you think prison is any better the longer you're inside?' grumbled the penis, reading her thoughts. 'What kind of life is it for anyone, being allowed out only for a few minutes in the bathroom and at night when the lights are off?'

The man did not offer her his hand to climb the stile. He was on the other side of the lane, looking round. In a moment he found his bearings and his back straightened. 'This way,' he said. 'And when we get to the water meadows we'll stop for tea.'

For the mile and a half along the public lane the penis kept quiet. Perhaps it feared discovery by a third party. But in the long grass near the river where the man unscrewed the thermos it became persistent again, even querulous. She touched it in friendship through his jeans and it moved and grew engagingly bulbous in response.

'For God's sake,' said the voice of either the man or the penis. 'Let's get on with it.'

It was the man who had spoken. She stood up. He shouldered his rucksack and they continued downhill.

'Anyone could see us there,' said the man. 'We'll find somewhere later.'

The penis laughed. 'I told you I was the boss. He's only walking to get where I want to go. I'm always leading him on, thrusting into places where he can't go, exploring smooth, slippery caverns and ridges from which he is barred by his bulk. You've no idea how he envies me.'

She giggled again. The man, interpreting this as nervous anticipation, put his hand on her waist and left it there until it made walking too awkward.

'Have you heard the one about the cock that had two chickens?' asked the penis and went on to tell a dirty joke, the most salacious of punchlines slipping easily from its absent tongue.

The man led the way across a wooden bridge and into a pine plantation where, sure enough, it was easy to step aside from the waymarked path, to slip between the dark trees and out into a sunny clearing occupied only by crickets scratching their legs in the tall, seeding grass.

She sat down. The rough grass brushed the skin of her arms and legs. The stalks around her were warm and so high she could see nothing beyond but the sky. At their tips were so many different kinds of seeds: a tight-lipped plume, a thin, ridged blade, others frothy and tinged with pink and the commonest a dull beige, loose and ready to be blown away.

'Ideal,' said the man. 'Not a soul in sight.' He sat down beside her.

She said 'Hello' to the penis when the man undressed and the penis said 'Hello' back. Contrary to expectation it made no move in her direction but started to explore its surroundings with a zest which pulled the man to his feet, this way and that way as though he were walking a large, untrained dog and being jerked, from the end of the leash, towards new seductive smells. She propped her elbow on her knee, her chin on her hand and watched through the tasselled grass as the pair of them moved across the clearing.

The penis set off in a new direction between ranks of resinous trees. She followed. Soon shade gave way to sun again, the trees to fragrant hedgerow, hedgerow to a meadow where all the flowers of childhood bloomed.

The man was lost. He unfolded the map to help him. A warm breeze lifted it over his face. The penis thrust forward and the man, naked except for the map, stumbled behind.

It was at this point that the penis began to sing in a pleasant baritone 'Green Grow the Rushes O!' – something easy and popular so everyone could join in.

The man spoke but his voice kept fading into the background. She could distinguish a word or two but not whether his words made sentences, instructions or demands.

'Hang about,' she said to the penis. She knelt down and picked daisies for a chain to adorn her new friend. 'Do you like butter?' she asked, raising a buttercup to see its reflection. Then she rose and they went on. 'I'll sing you one O!' sang the penis. 'What is your one O?' she sang in response.

'Contour lines, footbridge, tumulus, bridleway,' the man gabbled into his map.

'Be quiet,' she said. 'One is one and all alone and ever more shall be so,' she sang in harmony with the penis as they meandered down the sunny green hill, while the man, struggling to keep the map off his face, blundered after them.